MISTRESS OF THE DAMNED

&

DEATH IN HER ARMS

TWO TALES OF MURDER AND PASSION

by

CHARLES NUETZEL

WRITING AS "GEORGE FREDRICS"

The Borgo Press
An Imprint of Wildside Press

MMVII

FIRST COMBINED EDITION

CONTENTS

Introduction 5

BOOK ONE: MISTRESS OF THE DAMNED

Chapter One 9
Chapter Two..19
Chapter Three..29
Chapter Four 37
Chapter Five 51
Chapter Six..65
Chapter Seven 77

BOOK TWO: DEATH IN HER ARMS

Prologue 87
Chapter One 89
Chapter Two..101
Chapter Three..111
Chapter Four 123
Chapter Five 129
Chapter Six..135
Chapter Seven 143
Epilogue 159

About the Author 164

INTRODUCTION

This book is two short novels in one; more bang for the buck, so they say in promo copy. Well, each was too short to make a full-size edition, so I said: double up, more fun for all concerned.

Both books have seen print previously in different forms. They are, in the present edition, somewhat modernized and "run past the author's eyes" for a last revision. Ah, how wonderful that can be. In a case like this, it is a chance to look at things from a different perspective, from a more "mature" point of view.

Authorities on writing have said time and time again: revise, revise, revise. Writing is rewriting. Do your first, second, and final draft on a story and simply file it away for another day. Let it mellow and simmer down, and let your mind climb out of the state of mad ecstasy that made it possible to set down on paper your golden words. And what horrors you'll discover the next time you pick up your "great artistic masterpiece."

Sure, nice advice, and certainly a necessary part of the creative process. But what does one do when under the demands of making a living at the writing game and meeting hard to deal with deadlines? You write, doing the best job you can, and send it off in time to meet publisher's demands.

And you have to live with the end result.

Well, it is either that or endlessly sitting before the typewriter and hammering over every word of the opening line until one is satisfied that it is in the very best possible condition!

Of course, under those circumstances, ya put it in the drawer and pick it up a few days later when you're in a cooler creative mood, and darn if those "golden words" don't need total revision, or maybe even a total cut forever more.

Thus writing is a continual matter of making decisions one has to live with for the rest of their lives, like some condemned criminal!

Well, sometimes fate takes a turn and offers up a second chance and the writer can start fresh—within the given limits of deadlines to meet publisher's demands!

And so they are now presented.

—CHARLES NUETZEL
Thousand Oaks, California
July 2006

BOOK ONE

Mistress of the Damned

MISTRESS OF THE DAMNED; &, DEATH IN HER ARMS

CHAPTER ONE

Bryon Silvers stood like a thin pole behind his large, neatly arranged desk, his body seemingly too small for his gray suit. A thick, oversize cigar was clamped between his thin lips. His dark eyes bore into Paul Phillips.

After a moment he said: "Sit, boy!"

The cigar snapped out of his mouth and he pointed it toward a chair opposite his, across the desk. Reaching for a small intercom, he flipped a switch and said: "Get Jack!"

Paul took his time sitting in the small, awkward chair. He took a cigarette, lit it and dragged deeply, trying to look relaxed and casual. His nerves were tense, waiting to see what would follow. He felt like a man in the den of a vicious lion, about to be attacked. He let his eyes examine Silvers'. He had come face to face with Bryon Silvers in the man's office the day before and at the party when the man had introduced him to Lynn.

Bryon smiled; it was merely a movement of his lips, without humor and without emotions—his eyes were cold; examining. "You like Lynn?"

"Of course—but I don't like a spy strapped to my back!"

"She told you that?" Bryon demanded.

"No—it was obvious! I do business with the man not..."

Bryon snapped him short with: "That doesn't matter. I like to know the kind of man I'm doing business with. Since I have the money and I am offering the job—you do it my way. Understand?" The cigar stabbed out at him.

"Don't start bullying me," Paul warned in a mild voice. "I don't push easily."

9

Silence answered him.

A few moments later, Bryon Silvers laughed. "Maybe you'll be all right, after all!"

Just then the door opened and a large, heavy man stepped into the room. His eyes snapped to Paul and showed immediate dislike.

"Jack Myer—Paul Phillips—you two'll work together on this deal!" Silvers announced. "Take a chair."

Without saying a word, Jack Myer sat next to Paul.

Silvers grinned as if at a personal joke. "You know, Jack, Lynn says he's all right." It was a needling remark.

Jack's face jerked toward Paul's, his eyes narrowed, filled with strong emotion.

"Jack likes Lynn—but she don't go for him." Silvers shrugged and then laughed once more as if it were a great joke. "Well, enough of this. We have a job to do." He turned his attention to Paul.

"Two trips for a thousand each—plus expenses. So the G-note will be pure gravy."

"What do I have to do for the 'gravy'?"

"Just pilot your plane and don't ask questions. Jack will take care of everything." The cigar stabbed the air with every word.

"Where to?"

"Mexico. Contact is being made with certain people who want to buy something we have to offer."

"What?"

Silvers' eyes narrowed and his lips compressed over the cigar. After a moment he said: "You don't have to concern yourself with that! Just do the work you're hired for—and you get the money afterwards."

"Half before and half afterwards," Paul countered.

Silvers looked surprised and then nodded. "Five hundred before the first flight and five hundred on the return. The second thousand after the second trip."

Paul nodded, asked: "When is the first flight?"

"Tomorrow."

"Where to in Mexico?"

"A small ranch—you'll be given the destination tomorrow at the air field. Okay?" Silvers stood. "All arrangements will be made in advance for the flight. You don't need any more information at this time." He extended his hand, indicating the meeting was over.

Paul stood, taking the other's hand. "What time?"

"Lynn will let you know...you are planning to be with her, aren't you?"

Jack Myer started to say something, his eyes burning at Paul.

Paul nodded.

"Then don't worry about anything. She'll keep you informed."

Annoyed, Paul stepped from the office. A little later he was outside. He stood there in the blinding sun. For a long time he was undecided. Then his roving eyes spotted a cocktail lounge.

Half an hour later with two Martinis playing in his brain, Paul got into his car and drove to the small airport where his two-engine plane was homed.

Restlessness settled over him, which could only be calmed by finding his way into the clouds, away from the world of reality and its problems. It was only a matter of minutes to check through the Mary-Lou and fill her tank, warm her up and start her down the airstrip.

It had been a little over a week since he'd flown, and a feeling of excitement settled over him as the plane slowly lifted from the field and made its way skyward.

He didn't like Bryon Silvers. A gnawing feeling that this job was going to wind up a mess stayed with him. The secrecy was unsettling. He knew nothing about Bryon Silvers except what he had heard. Which was so damned little.

Silvers was a high pressure businessman who was involved in many shady dealings. The question was, how dangerous might it be for himself? Yet, he needed the money, and fast. Otherwise there would be no plane, no business, nothing. And he had been making his living for some time with the Mary-Lou.

But all that slowly faded in importance. The questions became almost meaningless, the doubts only plaguing against the idea of losing his plane. He'd been in tight situations before, and there would be many others in his life.

Hell, Paul thought angrily, *you've gotten into messes many times.*

Paul directed the plane into the clouds and then slipped out into the bright sunlight. Tipping the plane's wing, he circled in a slow curve, looking down at the world below. Tiny dots of city activity spread out beneath him like an anthill.

All those people sweating it out for nothing but a tired old existence, he thought, suddenly happy at the freedom, which he was now feeling.

Life pins you down like a struggling bug, sticks you to the glue of sweat and toil, and what do you come up with but a few moments of painful pleasure, captured in a moment's forgetfulness.

That was life down there.

But here in the sky, freedom blanketing around him on all sides, nothing mattered, no thought was truly important, no problem of importance to plague him.

He didn't have to think about the kind of person he was. He didn't have to worry about the next action, the next bend in his road of life.

He was his own man here, in complete control of his destiny.

His thoughts suddenly drifted to Lynn Palmer.

Bryon had introduced him to Lynn during the blastout party at the man's large expensive house. Drinks flowed heavily that night and the crowd of people fairly bumped into each other, sometimes with half-staggering motion, as they milled from one room to another. Lynn had immediately attached herself to Paul, after the swift introduction. Two drinks, followed by some very close dancing was enough to close the deal. Her body was flush against his, her hips gently surging in a blatantly seductive way. And her lips were so close, under his. She smiled as if to say, *I know what you want!* Or maybe just: *we both want the same thing.* But the message was communicated very gracefully by the warm invitation in her lovely eyes. To accent all that, she literally pressed a light kiss on his lips at the close of the dance. It was a very unsubtle pass, and made the point.

"Want to split?" he asked, taking her hand in his, and

12

leading the way through the room.

"I don't think you're giving me any choice, are you?" she murmured with a light throaty laugh. "My, aren't you the joy!"

Nothing more was said about that as they left house. Once outside, though, Lynn merely informed him: "I have a place not far from here. Okay?"

Twenty minutes later they were at her apartment. One glance into the living room solidified Paul's first suspicions. The apartment was expensively furnished. An original seascape hung over the fireplace. A bar divided the living room from the dining area.

"This is where we carry on our 'fun and games'!" Lynn softly laughed. "Let's have something to drink."

Paul looked into her dark green eyes. He wondered why such an attractive woman would play around with the Silvers' group; a group that was thick with toughs, characters, tramps, and prostitutes. As she glided across the room he found it a delightful study in sensual teasing to watch her. The wide full hips jerked with every movement; but in a classy way, rather than a cheap whorish manner. As she leaned forward for the whiskey and glasses, her low-cut blouse revealed a brimming bust. It was a wonderful, exciting view.

At least, Silvers had set a real super lady on him—regardless of his motives.

"Bryon Silvers wanted you to bring me here, didn't he?" Paul inquired, taking a sip of the whiskey which she had handed him. His eyes found it hard to keep away from her hefty neckline.

"Something like that," she admitted, looking directly into his eyes.

"What's the pitch?" he asked, "Just entertainment—or something else?"

Lynn was thoughtful for a moment. Her full red lips suggested a kiss as they pursed up. "You wouldn't want me to tell stories out of school, would you?"

He laughed, then shrugged. "I guess not."

But the implication of her words had been enough to suggest the truth of his suspicions. But one couldn't blame the man. After all, the job was a good one—pay-wise, and it would hold a lot of responsibility, in its way. Maybe this was his way to sizing up a man.

* * * * * * *

Much later, lying back on the bed, Paul discovered himself wondering about the events, which now brought him to this point in his life. Bryon Silvers was known to have been involved in shady deals and now he wanted the use of Paul's twin engine plane. Mortgage payments on the plane were long past due and he urgently needed a couple of thousand dollars or he'd lose the little that he had left in the world. He would normally have steered clear of this deal but he needed money right now and this seemed the only way.

Restlessly he turned and looked at the woman lying next to him.

His eyes roved along her body, which had given him so much pleasure only a few moments before. She was a lovely female, large, the way he had always liked them; strong and demanding in her love-making.

There was a quiet class about her, strangely enough. Maybe it was more a style.

Lynn stirred and her eyes jerked suddenly open, staring up at him. For a moment no expression showed on her features.

Then slowly a smile, warm, pleased, moved her lips, and she said: "I knew I'd like you, Paul. I just knew it from the first moment. Sometimes that happens when you see a person for the first time. It's..." she thought for a moment, then snapped her fingers—"Instant sex!"

"Lynn—how'd you happen to get into this kind of life?" he questioned.

"Being a tramp?" she asked, unembarrassed. Yet there was a sharp edge of bitterness and self hate flavoring her words.

He shrugged; wishing it was possible to withdraw the question.

"Oh, don't be embarrassed. I know what I am. I've learned to face it—regardless of what that might be. I'm a

14

lush, too! Maybe that's my only redeeming feature."

"Lynn—you don't have to—"

She shook her head, saying: "No—we might as well get off on the right foot...I'm what I am because things worked out that way and I had too much pride to just turn tail and return to my home town, settle down and marry some slob and raise little brats.

"Don't get me wrong—I love children and all that— but, with the right man. The idea of marrying some cat that I don't respect and having his brood—well, I don't like that idea any more than facing old friends and admitting what I turned out to be."

She sat up, reached for a pack of cigarettes on the bedstand, took one and handed him another. Taking a deep drag, she continued: "I'd rather drown my sorrow in booze and.... Well, 'fun and games'."

She laughed almost bitterly.

Paul found his hand reaching out instinctively toward hers, squeezing it. "Aren't you a little harsh on yourself?"

Her eyes jerked to his, amazed.

"Boy, aren't you the nice one? Well, thanks, anyway."

She lowered her gaze, took another deep drag and slowly let smoke drift past her parted lips.

Paul suddenly felt sorry for Lynn.

She looked up, eyes half-lidded, lips parted and moist, shining in the dim light of the moonlight which shone through the half open window on her side of the bed.

"You're really a nice guy—you should stay away from bastards like Bryon Silvers," she warned.

Lynn left the room a little while later and returned with two glasses of whiskey. She handed him one and then settled down next to him, gulping from her own drink. She turned and looked at Paul.

"I told you my story—how about yours?"

Paul hesitated and then shrugged. "Isn't much."

"You don't want to talk about it?" she sounded disappointed.

"Sure, why not?" he laughed. "What do you want to know?"

15

"Why you are teaming up with Silvers."

"I'm not teaming up with him. He just has a job for me."

"That'll be the day when he lets a guy do business with him only once," she warned, finishing off her drink.

"Maybe I'll be the first. I learned about his needing a plane at the air field where I park my crate. This one job is to get me out of hock!"

"That's what they all say."

She pursed her lips and then added: "I'm almost tempted to tell him not to do business with you—for your sake."

Paul tensed. He had been right about Lynn after all. "I need the cash. Desperately. What can I do to...get a good report card?"

"Forget it. I'll give a good report on you, in the morning. I was just thinking out loud."

"Then you were to feel me out?"

"Sure thing," she admitted brightly, "but do me a favor and please don't tell him I've told you."

"What makes you think I can be trusted?"

She laughed. "A girl can tell about men. You're tight lipped. Not the type to tell stories out of school." Lynn shrugged her shoulders. "Don't say I didn't warn you, Paul."

"Don't worry, I can handle myself," he assured her.

Lynn's eyes ran over the large muscles of his shoulders, the expanse of his chest, and the flat hardness of his stomach.

"I bet you can. Just watch out for another man that can handle himself pretty good, too—Jack Myer. He's Silvers' hatchet man."

Paul was annoyed with the conversation.

Lynn sensed his mood and reached for him, drawing him very near her.

There wasn't any conversation after that.

Paul woke to hear humming as Lynn dressed in the far corner of the room.

"About time you woke," she scolded. "It's ten."

Paul jerked up in bed, startled. "I gotta get out of here. Silvers is expecting me at his office in thirty minutes,"

16

he cried in a worried voice.

He started to get dressed. Out of the corner of his eye he caught Lynn watching him, a sad expression on her face.

"You'll be back?" she inquired.

"I thought you were following orders, bringing me here."

Lynn shook her head. "Not completely. I didn't have to go that far. I could have told him in minutes that you'd be a closed-mouth guy."

There wasn't time for more than a promise to meet at her place at seven, a quick kiss and then good-bye.

She had been damned good for him. In his time Paul had known a lot of women, but there was something about Lynn that was different. He'd always been an all-day sucker for a beautiful broad with a sad story. That had been his trouble right from the beginning.

Paul decided it would be rather nice being with Lynn this evening.

MISTRESS OF THE DAMNED; &, DEATH IN HER ARMS

CHAPTER TWO

Lynn opened the door on the second ring and stepped back, feeling a gnawing sick sensation as she looked at the man who walked into her apartment.

Jack Myer.

Terror whipped through her. But there was nothing she could do about it. Jack was a strong, nasty, dangerous man. Right from the beginning she'd been frightened by him. And that fear had caused her to do things that might, in time, protect her—but right now, in private with the man, there wasn't much recourse but to play his game, his way.

"Hello, baby," the guy greeted, stripping her body with his eyes.

Lynn was dressed in a tight fitting skirt and tighter sweater. It was the kind of outfit that pleaded for a man's caressing looks. It demanded a man's eyes. But it was not the kind of outfit that she wanted Jack Myer to see her in. She didn't want him to look at her in that way—ever.

Yet there wasn't anything she could do about the situation; there never had been anything she could do about Jack Myer except let the man have his way—to a point.

Not after that first brutal time with this beast. She felt like a cheap whore thinking about it. The only thing that made it possible to deal now was the realization that it wouldn't be too long before everything blew up in the bastard's face. Then harsh revenge would be fully dished out for what he'd done to her.

Lynn forced a smile and then asked, "Want a drink, first?" she offered, making her voice sound inviting.

There could be only one reason why Jack would come to her apartment, and that reason was sex. And he was in the position to make his desires a demand.

"Why not?" he grinned, devouring her savagely with his eyes.

Lynn stepped away and then walked into the kitchen. The man followed her and as she reached for a bottle of whiskey, which was on the top shelf of the cupboard, Jack came up behind her, crushing her back against his chest. She could feel his rather bold reaction with that blunt physical contact. He tried to slide his hands around to her breast, but she playfully stepped away, turning.

It was the kind of action she might enjoy with somebody like Paul, but Myer—no!

"You want a drink, or free thrills?" she inquired, frantically trying to fight down the ebbing well of revulsion building deep inside her.

"Both!" the man laughed.

Oh, how she hated this man—how she would almost do anything to get rid of him, for good. Right now. But she'd been warned to play along—wait a little while, let things settle down, let events run their course.

Damned easy for them *to say!* She thought, bitterly, wanting to ram a glass down the man's throat or smash a hammer up his crotch.

He was the only creature in the world that she really wished would drop dead—and soon. But this wasn't the time to yank the rug out from under him. Yet it wouldn't be long. They'd promised her that much. Still, right at this very moment wouldn't be soon enough. The only thing that kept her under control was realizing that the nightmare would soon end. Then he'd learn the price of fooling around with her—and many of the other women who were used as toys for his brutal demands. But for now she had to go along—bide her time.

"You got some body. It never stops. I kinda dig you, Lynn. A lot—a real lot! Love those jugs you have. Bouncy ouncies! Makes a man really itch!"

Lynn ignored his words, opened the bottle of whiskey, reached for a couple of glasses and then poured two stiff drinks.

She would need some stiff boozing to make it possible to go through with the bedroom scene with Jack Myer. If only there was some way out of it!

Turning, she handed the man one glass and then took a long hungry swallow from her own glass.

Her life had become a cesspool of pleasing slobs like this. But most of them were at least human. How could a nice girl like her get into such a horrid mess? And she couldn't blame anybody but herself.

Someday it would be impossible to stand letting this man have his way with her. And she dreaded that moment.

The man's eyes appraised her body, as if literally feasting on her flesh.

"Why don't you take that stuff off? I like to look at your boobs all nice and naked like. You know how I am!"

"I know!" she muttered, finding it difficult to avoid the contempt from showing.

"Well, rip it off, babe! I can't wait all day. Little daddy here wants to play!" He grinned evilly like a demon from hell. "And these wanna play, too!" He bounced his hands, palms up, while staring hungrily at her breasts. "Like they say in the strip shows, take it off, take it off, take it all off, babe!"

It was a command.

Everything Jack Myer said was in the form of a command, and if Lynn wanted to get along, she'd learned it was necessary to do exactly as the man ordered. He could be brutal with those hands, hitting a woman senseless.

"Take it off take it off, I wanna fill my hands with ya, babe!" he literally sang in a monotone.

Sick inside, fighting to keep her emotions in control, forcing back the tears of shame and disgust, she shrugged her shoulders.

"Anything to make you're little toy happy!" she muttered, thinking of all the other words, which were a far better fit.

Putting down the glass, Lynn pulled the sweater over her head.

He stepped back some and continued to stare at her. It was a dirty jungle animal look of pure passion and desire.

"How'd the new man make out?" Lynn asked conversationally.

"Okay, I guess," Jack said in a dry voice which indicated that he really wasn't even aware of what the conversation was about.

"What's the bit with him?" she pushed.

"Fly-boy for some guns. Down Mexico way. For some South American hard noses who want to make a take-over of their country!"

Jack laughed again, this time even more sensually. "I don't want conversation, baby. I came here to play ball with your balloons!" He laughed almost hysterically at that. "And you sure got them nice, well rounded, so full and firm and fully packed double scoops! I dream of being just smothered…a nightmare of joy…last night! And I came here to make my dream come true."

She'd love to smother him to death, if that was possible! One phone call was all she needed. But not now. Not yet.

"I don't want no more talking about that fly-boy. Don't like him! Let's move! In there. So I can make use of your body. I need it. Boy do I need it, now. Get out of that other stuff! I want the whole meal, served up as a full treat to eat! Just laying there on your big, beautiful bed! Oh, how I dig that hot bod!"

* * * * * * *

The sun was setting when Paul turned the plane back toward the field. The landing was made in semi-darkness.

He had been thinking about Lynn Palmer during much of the flight. He taxied the plane into its allotted spot and got out. A few moments later he was behind the wheel of his car, driving toward Lynn's apartment. It was some twenty minutes' drive to her place, and every minute was feeding more and more excitement through him. Surprisingly enough he felt a strange connection with her. Maybe they were a couple of people who just happened to click—in a friendly way. Of course, the woman was a knockout.

As he was walking down the hall toward her apartment, the door suddenly opened and Jack Myer stepped out.

The man saw Paul, but said nothing as he hurried past.

Paul moved to the still-open door.

"Anybody home?" he called.

There was silence for several seconds, then Lynn answered: "Who is it?"

"Paul Phillips."

"Come on in, the door's open."

He stepped into the living room, closing the door behind him. Lynn wasn't there. He guessed she might be in the bedroom and stepped toward it. Then on second thought he turned and walked to the sofa, sat slowly down, fighting the almost overpowering desire to go into the bedroom and make a forward, direct pass.

He wondered what Jack Myer had wanted with Lynn. An edge of anger jabbed at him at the thought of what Myer might have wanted from Lynn. The idea of Myer sharing the same room, let alone the same bed with her caused a rush of disgust to race through Paul.

Just then Lynn Palmer stepped into the room. She was dressed in a house coat, he was sure she had nothing else on.

"Hello, you're early," she greeted. Stepping over to Paul and leaning down, she brushed her lips gently against his.

"I didn't know there was any specific time we agreed upon."

"Want a drink?" she offered, smiling warmly, her eyes bright and tender as they looked into his.

"Could use one, I guess."

"Hard day at the office?" She stepped to the bar. "Well, difficult might be a better word. Hard has so many meanings!"

Paul laughed. "Went smoothly. And all that."

She returned with two drinks, handing him one.

He asked: "What was the visit about?"

"Jack?" When he nodded, she continued:

"Something personal!"

But there was a harsh bitterness to her voice, which he didn't miss.

They sat sipping their drinks, saying nothing. Paul

23

was trying to think of a way to question Lynn about the business with Bryon Silvers. Strangely it was Lynn who brought up the subject, as if guessing his thoughts.

"I hear everything went pretty well, from their side. What do you think about Bryon?"

"Don't know, to be honest. Maybe you could tell me something."

"Out of school?" she giggled. It was obvious that she was feeling her liquor. He guessed it wasn't this drink in her hands now. Apparently she had had several before he'd arrived.

"Out of school," he suggested, probing her face for a reaction.

"Well, he's a no-good bastard, if you want the honest truth. That's one point. Point two, he does business just under the thin line of the law, if you know what I mean. Nobody has been able to even touch him, because he's smart enough to be very careful. He has lawyers covering every move he makes.

"But I guess you know about all that—or at least I assume you're intelligent enough to guess it."

Paul shook his head slowly from side to side. "To be truthful, I know very little about the man."

"The less you know about Bryon, the better off you are going to be," she announced firmly.

Silence.

Then: "What's this deal all about, Lynn...I've been kept in the dark Nobody tells me much of anything."

She smiled for a moment, then frowned. "You aren't supposed to know."

She was quiet for a moment, then slowly nodded, as if thinking to herself. Finally she said:

"Smuggling, dope, or illegals? I don't now for sure. Whatever. Just...well...best not to ask questions."

His expression must have revealed his shock at her announcement.

"Chicken out?" she quickly asked, almost as if she hoped he would. She sat down next to him.

"No. What kind of smuggling?" he inquired, trying to sound as casual as possible, trying to hide the grinding fear which ate its way through his nerves. "Better that than opening doors for possible terrorists!"

"I wouldn't worry about that part. Just guns to would-be revolutionists, for a South American revolt—or something like that. Good money in it. That's why he needs a plane like…well—your plane."

"I'd think he'd have had one before now."

"Did, but lost it last time around. Don't know the details—but it's enough to know he needed a new man. And fast. You happened to be hanging loose in the wind. Looks like you're the one. Want to walk out, now? I could arrange it, you know." She pleaded with him with her eyes.

"What side are you on?" Paul asked, uneasily.

"There aren't sides. I play things down the middle and do what I damned please." She thought for a moment and then added: "I don't know why I care about you—but I do."

She laughed at that. "Sounds like a song title."

Paul realized that she was either drunk or pretty close to it. He pushed his advantage.

"Who's Silvers doing business with?"

"I don't know. That's something he keeps to himself and hatch-face Jack Myer." Bitterness, anger and pain broke across her features. Her hand tightened on the tall glass, the fingers whitening. "How I hate that bastard!"

Paul felt embarrassment. He took another swallow of whiskey. His eyes slowly returned to Lynn. She was a mixture of lush maturity and a little bit of young child. Not innocent, but intelligent. And merely lost human. Much like himself, perhaps. They were alike in that manner. And something about her that hid behind a hard shell, which was very vulnerable. Just like a little lost child. Paul realized then that regardless of everything else Lynn might be, he couldn't help feeling a deep closeness to her, an emotional tie that had nothing to do with their physical relationship. And little to do with rational logic. He wanted to protect her. He wanted to place an arm around her shoulder, draw her close, in a caring manner of a friend. It was so easy being with the woman.

Without meaning to be seductive or making a pass, he let his arm fold about her, and draw her close. She hesi-

25

tated for a moment, not resisting so much as uncertain as to his motivations. Then she came closer, resting her head on his shoulder. They sat there for a very long time, not speaking, just being aware of one another, like lost friends redefining their relationship.

And that redefinition suddenly smoldered hot. When he turned, leaned down to kiss her, it was with a strange sense of affection, tenderness. When their lips met it was soft, gentle fire, which almost instantly surged into utter fury as their mouths opened to one another. After that there was no stopping. A volcano simply enveloped them. After that first, prolonged kiss they were driven beyond control. They took to one another like to a savage jungle, unable to contain the power that drove their bodies into an instant mating. Only later would they move to the bedroom to rediscover one another in a slower, more lingering manner, touching, caressing, and lovingly rediscovering one another. But on the sofa it was wanton passion totally overwhelming everything else in a blaze unrelenting passion.

* * * * * * *

Lynn Palmer woke him at eight in the morning. Breakfast was waiting when he came into the kitchen—three fried eggs, basted in butter, three pieces of bacon, a large cup of steaming hot coffee and a triple shot of whiskey to wash it all down.

Finishing the last of the whiskey, he looked at Lynn, letting his eyes run along the flow of blonde hair, which rested on her shoulders.

He returned his gaze to her face. "What'd I do to deserve all this?"

Lynn shrugged, grinning happily. "Let's say you're the first guy to treat me like a lady. Anyway, I thought you could use something to pick you up. You have a hard couple of days ahead of you, Paul."

"When does it all start?"

"Nine AM."

Paul looked at his watch. "God, ten minutes to go. I take it somebody is coming here to meet me."

26

Lynn lowered her eyes. "Yes, Jack."

Paul pulled her into his arms, thrilling to the pure softness of that curved against his body.

"Oh, Paul, take care," she told him. They slowly released one another and sat down at the breakfast table.

Paul was about to say something when the doorbell rang.

Lynn jerked to her feet, startled, then quickly disappeared into the living room.

A minute later she returned with Jack Myer.

"Well, ain't this cozy," the man observed nastily, his eyes filling with hate as they turned toward Paul.

"Let's lay off the personal stuff, Jack," Lynn suggested.

"Don't tell me what to do!" he warned, taking a threatening step towards her.

Paul stood, barred the other man's way.

"Simmer down, boy!" he ordered, tapping the man on the chest.

The two of them stared at each other. Hate built stronger in Jack Myer's eyes. It looked as he was about to attack Paul, then he suddenly relaxed, grinned coldly. "Don't push too hard fly-boy! We gotta get along together."

"Boys, boys, why don't you act like adults?" Lynn suggested, stepping between them, frowning with concern, her eyes seemed haunted as she quickly looked at Paul.

"Yeah," Jack suggested, laughing, "Let's be adults. Maybe we should get on your bed for a double whammy at that body of yours!"

"Screw off!" Paul snapped, grabbing the man's shoulders. "Don't you ever even think?"

Jack laughed in his face. "You sure are a sucker, man! Has she got you twisted around her bod? Well, good luck to you! What is he, number ten thousand?"

"Knock it off," Paul warned. "Just try to be a nice little gentleman. If you know how!"

"Sure do. With a lady, that is!" Jack snapped back.

Lynn broke in, then, saying: "Now boys, be nice. No sense in fighting over me, flattering as it might sound."

Her eyes pleaded with Paul, behind Jack's back, to

simmer down.

Paul forced a smile and extended his hand toward the other man. "I'm willing. Better that we get along, okay?"

Myer ignored the offering after staring coldly at the outstretched hand.

"We gotta get on the ball. We leave in a few hours," Jack announced. "Just the two of us. Here—" He reached into his jacket pocket and pulled out an envelope, handing it to Paul. "This is the first installment, as promised. Do what you're paid for and nothing will go wrong with our plans for the next payments." There was a ringing threat his hard voice.

"When do we return?"

"Tomorrow," was the bullet type answer.

Lynn turned to Paul, asking: "You'll see me when you get back?"

"Sure, of course, darling," Paul said, putting it on thick for Jack Myer's sake.

Lynn's eyes sparkled as she put her hand on his shoulder and then leaned close to kiss his cheek.

Jack's eyes followed the action, squinting; his lips twitched.

"Get the ball rolling, fly-boy! Come on!" Jack demanded irritated.

Paul drew Lynn tighter against him, covering her lips with his own. She opened her lips to his kiss, boldly underscoring the obvious meaning of their mutual pleasure in one another. The action, which was intended to annoy the other man, succeeded.

Jack Myer watched and the hard, hateful expression burning in his eyes said it all: if given a chance he'd probably kill Paul.

CHAPTER THREE

They flew over the Mexican border some time after one in the afternoon. Jack Myer had kept himself occupied in the back compartment, which had a small table and seats for seven passengers. Paul was glad to be alone, to think his own thoughts. He'd half expected the other man to sit in the co-pilot's seat—an idea which was far from appealing to Paul.

During the flight his thoughts drifted to Lynn Palmer, and they were strangely tender thoughts. Maybe it was her brazen attitude about life, her honesty, her concern about him, even if she was from outward appearances a tramp. First impressions could be false. People were simply far too complex to be defined in one word.

Jack Myer, coming into the pilot's compartment, cut his thoughts short.

"Let me take over, now," the man ordered.

Paul jerked as if he had been shot, then moved his head toward Jack, staring coldly into the other's hard eyes.

"What the hell you talking about?"

"I fly."

"Not this plane, you don't!" Paul assured him.

Silence answered Paul and then Jack Myer settled down into the co-pilot's seat.

"Don't touch those controls!" Paul warned.

"Lay off, fly-boy, or you're in trouble—big trouble. I won't touch your damned plane—if that's the way you want it. But you had better follow directions!"

"That's what I'm being paid for. Nobody but nobody flies Mary-Lou except me. That's 'company' policy!"

Jack Myer told Paul to make a broad circle while he examined the area beneath them.

"Pull her around, return to course. It shouldn't be long now!"

Ten minutes later the man ordered him to drop lower.

"See that jetty—that series of rocks breaking the coastline up there?"

Paul nodded.

"Fly over them, circle and then you'll spot a landing strip marked on the beach."

Paul lowered the plane and at the proper time circled until he was in the right position for a landing, then gently dropped the plane's nose He glided down onto the long strip of white beach. As they were slipping out of their seats Paul spotted a group of men starting toward the plane A few moments later he followed Myer out of the plane.

"Hello, Jack," said a tall, handsome, olive-skinned man. He stepped up and shook hands with Myer. "I thought you wouldn't make it."

"Some days we get late starts, Mr. Santez."

Santez looked at Paul. "You must be Phillips."

Paul nodded, surprised that the man knew his name. "You have the advantage. Who're you?"

"That's none of your business, fly-boy," Jack announced nastily.

Santez frowned but said nothing. 'Well, come along, I'll take you to the bungalow."

Paul examined the four other men. They were hard looking, dark-skinned. And armed. He had seen their type in the Caribbean and Latin America.

He followed them across the sand to the strip of jungle that covered the land behind. There was a well-marked trail through the undergrowth and twenty yards farther they came to a clearing. In the middle stood a large one-story bungalow with red tile roof. They walked toward the building and then onto the large comfortable porch and into the huge living room, which was furnished in Old World, handmade furniture.

Money radiated from every inch of the room. In the far corner was a small cabinet, which displayed a large supply of liquor.

"Let's have some drinks and then get down to business," Santez suggested in his lightly accented voice.

Drinks were handed around—rum and lime juice, chilled in tall glasses.

It was strong but pleasant tasting.

"How're things in your country?" Jack inquired of Santez.

"Miserable! That's why we want to change things around a bit. It's about time the common man got his chance. We have the young students of all classes behind us. A tyrant rules the government! He's—"

"I wouldn't talk too much detail," Jack Myer warned, motioning toward Paul

"Oh, I didn't know."

There was a long awkward silence while they finished their drinks Then Santez stood, looking politely at Paul, said "Help yourself to anything you might want while Mr. Myer and I arrange business details. I'll have Gina come out and keep you company."

He motioned Jack Myer to follow him and the other four men left with them.

Paul took a strong swallow of the rum and felt its contents slip down into his stomach. A few moments later the effects warmed his head

He was just finishing the drink when a small dark-haired woman stepped into the room walked to the bar and fixed herself a Rum & Coke.

He watched with growing interest.

She was wearing tight-fitting shorts that showed the line of her panties underneath. Slowly she turned and faced him, her smoldering large dark eyes studying him in detail. Her face was strikingly beautiful. The red of her lips was natural and unpainted. She stared at him for a long time in silence, her eyes appraising his large muscular form.

When she finally smiled, her full lips opened wide over even white teeth. Her eyes sparkled.

"I'm Gina," she announced. "Juan told me to keep you entertained."

The way Gina said the last word implied much more than conversation. The thought intrigued Paul.

It was so startling. Amazing. He hadn't expected to

31

be served any woman on a platter, let alone such a lovely, literally beautiful one.

He found his eyes caressing her figure. The white blouse open at the front revealed the deep crevice between her olive-colored breasts.

"You like me, much?" she inquired boldly, stepping across the room in a swivel-hipped fashion which was meant to create hot sparks. "Want a drink—help yourself!"

Paul looked at the empty glass in his hand and nodded. He mixed himself a large drink of rum and soda water. Then he turned and studied Gina.

He wondered what she was. House pet? Prostitute? Somebody's woman? Mistress of the house? What?

She stood there before a large window that faced an expensive patio beyond which was a guesthouse.

"What now?" he asked, nervously.

She faced him, her eyes flashing. "You didn't answer my question. Do you like me or don't you?"

"Why shouldn't I?" He sipped his drink and then hurriedly downed several quick swallows. He was already beginning to feel the liquor. He felt lightheaded and the obvious implication that this woman was his for the asking created an automatic surge of desire to rip through him.

She slowly nodded, then said: "What would you like to do?"

The sentence had all the obvious implications that she'd do anything he might like. His choice.

He let his eyes drift meaningfully over her figure. A slow burn crept through his nerves, like hot acid.

"Tell me, what's the real reason for your being sent to me?"

"There's going to be a long business meeting and they thought it better for you to be fully entertained—kept busy. That's what I'm for—keeping people busy—especially men. Want to go to my room?"

"Isn't this overdoing it a little?" Paul grinned.

"Why? Why shouldn't you be entertained? There's a long day and evening ahead—you might as well have something interesting to do. Santez keeps me around for such activities." Her bold statement held no self-pity; but rather an eagerness to entertain him. It wasn't personal, merely a matter of how things were for her. Gina's duty was, apparently, pleasing men. And, apparently, she was well rewarded for her "duties."

Paul shrugged, suddenly not really caring about the strange willingness of these people to keep him socially active with beautiful women. Probably they'd learned the best way to keep men satisfied and out of trouble was to throw in a nice beautiful woman to do a little private entertaining.

"Okay, let's split."

"Split?" her face was puzzled.

"Show me your room so we can find out what can happen. What can we do together for entertainment?"

"You don't know?" she asked, frowning.

He laughed at that. "I think I might be able to guess, if you gave me a hint."

He stepped to her and placed an arm around her waste. She leaned closer, smiled then and led the way out of the house, across the patio to the small bungalow.

Her room was tiny, with a large bed and dresser, leaving little room to move in. Nothing else, except bottles on the dresser.

"How you want it?" she asked quite businesslike, yet with a fire burning in her dark eyes.

Her cold, businesslike attitude had slapped ice across his face—regardless of the burn in her eyes. He stared at her, uneasy, nervous.

"How about a drink first?"

She told him to help himself.

As he was pouring a tall drink of whiskey, she lay on the bed. The liquor shot down his throat like hot fire. Paul slowly turned and looked at the woman. She was lying full length on the bed, her body displayed in such a way as to show off the full curves of her figure. She was a sensual jungle cat, all animal. Without a doubt a promising package there for him to open up.

"What you waiting for?" Gina inquired almost nervously.

He shrugged, but didn't move. He was mentally comparing Gina to Lynn and was startled by the dramatic difference. Where Gina and Lynn were both raw, savage sex, Lynn had a class about her, which was appealing, while Gina was a beautiful, voluptuous package of a Latin whoring sex. Direct, almost innocently so, but somewhat brazen in a totally impersonal way. Understandable. Yet still starkly different from Lynn, who had an undercurrent of class.

Paul shrugged, finished his drink and returned his attention to Gina. There was nothing else for him here at the plantation to do. And since she was there to please, he'd decided to make the most of it.

As he moved down to her, he found himself thinking about Lynn. For a brief moment he puzzled over that and then the excitement of Gina's hot body blurred all thoughts as she leaned into him, taking his hands and placing them under her blouse against her naked breasts. Her flesh was warm, soft and amazingly firm. She merely squirmed against him, then raised her arms, so the blouse lifted above her breasts. She smiled up at him, then took his head in her hands and literally pulled it down until he was smothering against her full, supple flesh.

"You have…such a hard body," she murmured, a few moments later, after having raced her hands all over him. "A hard man is good for a woman."

She started caressing his shirt off, and a moment later unbuckling his belt. Then helping him remove her shorts. After that things blurred into a sea of sensations, demanding actions that totally swallowed him into her embrace. She went directly into action, without so much as a word, yet her smile as she looked up at him was truly lustful. In moments it became obvious that Gina actually enjoyed being with a man. It was as if she couldn't get enough, and that lovely body just folded about him in every turn, legs, arms, lips and finally the very depths of her had captured him totally. The sounds that uttered from those full lips were real anguished pleasure, announcing the woman's total joy.

Paul was just submerged into fury of the woman's driving raw energy. She didn't stop until he was totally exhausted.

When he awoke, his body was bathed in sweat. He opened his eyes to discover he was alone. It was dark out-

34

side, and the night sounds of the tropic jungle sang softly in the distance. He stood and dressed, stepped to the dresser and fixed himself a drink. He downed the drink in two gulps and then went outside. He walked for a long time, thinking, wondering about what kind of arrangements had been made between Santez and Myer. He felt certain that whatever they were, they involved matters which would repel him. His thoughts slowly moved from Santez and Myer and drifted toward Lynn and then finally to the Latin sex bomb, Gina.

He wondered vaguely where Gina had gone. Finally he returned to Gina's room to find her lying on the bed.

"Brought food. Like beans? Tortillas?" She nodded to the dresser, on which was a tray. Suddenly he realized how hungry he actually was and devoured the meal she had brought. She seemed delighted with his enjoyment.

"You like?" she asked.

"Great! Just like you!" he chuckled. A quick, silent glance was exchanged, and then he moved down to her. He didn't want to think any more. He didn't want to think about Lynn or the Silvers job.

Paul found the escape he needed, but none of the contentment, which he'd hoped, would be there.

CHAPTER FOUR

The trip back from Mexico was a silent one. Jack Myer remained in the back compartment, uncommunicative. That suited Paul, perfectly.

A thick, rummy hangover was pounding his nerves raw, his stomach hated him, his eyes burned.

He felt as if he'd been dropped into a darkened, hole. The night with Gina had left him with a feeling of having slummed with a Main Street prostitute, regardless of how great a body she had!

Finally the trip ended and Paul returned to his apartment.

The next morning he awoke at eleven and showered. After dressing he called Bryon Silvers.

The secretary told him that Silvers was out and they'd get in touch with him when he was needed.

He fixed breakfast. While he was drinking his coffee his thoughts turned to Lynn Palmer. A strange powerful need burned at his guts for the woman he'd known for only a few days. It suddenly occurred to Paul that he hardly knew anything about her.

After finishing his coffee, he picked up the phone and dialed her number. There wasn't any answer. A strange sense of depression and restlessness set in as he put the receiver back on the phone.

In the next hours he tried to read. Several times he called Lynn's number. The very fact that she was unattainable made it more desirable to be with her. He smoked a lot and finally resorted to a drink to calm his nerves.

At five in the afternoon he called Lynn again, and this time she answered.

"I was wondering when you'd be getting home," he half scolded.

"Miss me?" Lynn inquired, sounding quite pleased.

"I've been trying to call you all afternoon. Where were you—I didn't think you worked for a living..."

"Now what's that supposed to mean?" Lynn snapped, emotion thick in her voice.

"I mean—I thought you have means of support." He felt like an ass for having said that. It was as much as calling her a whore: a kept woman. Nobody would stand still for that kind of remark, not even Lynn.

She hung up.

Paul stood there for a long time, the receiver in his hand. What was getting into him? Why should he care about a Lynn Palmer? She was just a little tramp—and he'd just called her what she was. But he realized that wasn't the complete picture, and he hated himself for having blundered so badly. Slowly he dialed the number again. The phone rang several times and then Lynn's voice asked who is it?

"Me again—please listen. I didn't mean that the way it sounded. It's just that I—"

The phone went dead and he was once more staring at the far wall. Paul angrily replaced the receiver and then left the apartment.

He walked for several hours, aimlessly, before he stepped into a steak house, had a cocktail and dinner. Afterwards he began walking again, this time in the direction of Lynn's apartment.

* * * * * * *

Lynn was sitting alone in her apartment, trying to get out of the depressed mood which had slammed over her after Paul's call.

It had hurt, all too much. More than she liked to think it could hurt her. But she'd been working on a hangover. And that could explain her sharp reaction. After all, he might honestly mean it differently. Maybe it hurt because it was so true. Several times she'd been tempted to call Paul and say she was sorry, but every time she thought of it another wave of hurt would cut through her like some knife was being sliced along her gut.

She had downed several strong drinks and was slightly high when the front door bell rang. For a moment a thrill shot through her.

Oh, if that could only be Paul, she thought, lunging toward the door. She swung the door open, ready to throw herself into Paul's arms.

Then a chill choked the warmth and hope that had poured into her. Jack Myer charged into the room, a leering grin spreading across his face. He slammed the door behind him and then turned, looked at Lynn; his eyes hot on her.

"Well, hello, little woman," he greeted, reaching out to touch her shoulder. Lynn twisted away.

Deep disappointment and depression hit her like a sledgehammer. The last person in the world she wanted to see was Jack Myer. The very idea of letting the man touch her body was just too much to stand.

"What's wrong, baby? Aren't you glad to see me?"

She choked down a retort that would have cut him down to size but good. Instead she merely said: "I'm hung over—if you know what I mean."

He reached for her, his hands clamping hard on her shoulders. "What's wrong?"

She struggled to get out of his grip, but the man held tight.

Panic rushed through Lynn. She remembered what it had been like the first time this man had forced her to his will. The memory didn't invite excitement in her. It was, also, a memory that brought a lot of conflicting emotions back into place.

"Please, Jack, I'm just not in the mood."

"What's with you? You whore! What right do you have to say that? Not in the mood. That has nothing to do with it. I'm in the mood, and that's all that counts. Sleep with a bastard like fly-boy and you don't want nothing of Jack, is that it?" he sneered, squeezing harder on her shoulders.

"Please give me a break, Jack," she pleaded, this time twisting with all her strength.

The suddenness of her move jarred her away from the

man. "Please, leave me alone," she cried, on the verge of tears and not knowing why.

"You whoring slut! You strip for every slob...what's with you and—"

"Stop calling me that!" she screamed, her fists doubling up at her side. The fury, the hurt, the almost overwhelming insanity of emotions choked at her reason. Most of all, she really hated the man.

Jack Myer took a threatening step toward her, a grin of pleasure cutting across his huge face. "You're a tramp—a slut—nothing...a little whore and the sooner you realize it the better it will be for you and—"

What made Lynn do it? She never would know. Suddenly her hand lashed out, hitting across his face in a stinging blow. She had wanted to do that and a lot more to this bastard. But what caused her to flare up at that exact moment, was another matter. The fury just surged up, overpoweringly.

"You goddamned bastard! Get the damned hell out of here before I kill you!" Lynn screamed at the top of her voice.

The grin, which spread wide on the man's face, sent terror through Lynn. Myer swung his right fist and she felt the impact of the blow that slammed her backwards, stunned. Pain jarred through her face and jaw. Red haze threatened her vision. Emotional agony ripped through her.

Then the man gripped her shoulders and hit her again.

* * * * * * *

Outside the apartment, Paul could just make out two shadowy figures framed against the window. From their actions it looked as if they were arguing. The larger one—apparently a man—was gesturing with his arms, then suddenly a fist lashed out at the smaller form. Fire raged through Paul. He wasn't even aware of running up the steps to Lynn's apartment.

Stopping in front of the door, he slammed his fist against it. A feeling of foolishness settled over him and he was about to leave when a muffled scream sounded from inside the apartment.

Paul rammed his shoulder against the door, smashing with all his weight and strength. The door made a crashing sound. He was backing up for another attack on the wooden barrier when the door suddenly flung open.

Jack Myer was standing there, his face beet-red, his eyes furious.

"What the hell you doing here?" the man demanded.

Before Myer could do anything, Paul rushed forward, pushing past him. He surveyed the room and saw that Lynn was sitting in a large chair, the side of her face marked with a red welt. A trickle of blood was starting to run down her chin.

"What are you doing—" was as far as Jack Myer got.

Paul whipped around, burying his fist deep into the man's gut. Myer staggered back, amazement blanching his features. Paul followed with a hard fist into the other's face. Blood gushed from his lips. Before Myer could recover, Paul attacked with two more brutal blows, one in the gut and another in the face.

Myer moaned and a shudder ran through his huge frame. He leaned forward, as if to return the attack, but Paul rabbit-punched the side of his neck. Paul grabbed the dazed and hurt man and shoved him out of the apartment. "You ever bother Lynn again and I'll beat your balls in! Got me?" Paul warned, slamming the door on the man's beaten face.

He turned and looked at Lynn. She was staring at him, open amazement on her face.

"What happened?" Paul asked, hurrying across the room.

Her face was wide with alarm and fear. She started to say something and then gasped in a deep breath.

"A drink?" she pleaded.

Paul walked to the bar, poured a strong shot of whiskey into a glass and then handed it to Lynn. She gulped it down and then asked for a cigarette.

"You shouldn't have done that," she told him.

Paul backed away, surprised. "1 didn't mean to cut into any business which wasn't—"

Lynn smiled crookedly and shook her head slowly from side to side. "I didn't mean it that way. Jack won't forget, that's all. He can get damned rough if he wants to," she told him. "Watch out. He'll get even. Real bad. He just might kill you for that!"

"I can take care of myself. And him."

"I saw that. But how many guys can you handle at a time?"

"Maybe he'll just let it go—figure he got off easy."

"Don't be silly. Just be careful. He might not try anything in the open—but if he gets a chance to get even, he will. Just believe me about that." A shudder shot through Lynn.

"So, I'll keep my eyes open. I think he's a coward. Harmless."

"Maybe?" was the answer. She was thoughtful and then asked: "Why'd you do it?"

"Are you kidding? I don't like men hitting women."

"That wasn't the only reason—was it?"

"No—I guess not," he admitted in a small voice.

Lynn nodded and then slowly stood, stepped to the bar, fixed herself a tall whiskey and took several swallows. "I'm sorry about this afternoon, Paul. You took me by surprise. I don't know why I was so childish."

"Forget it—it was my fault, anyway." He lighted a cigarette, asked. "What happened? Or isn't it my business?"

Lynn shrugged. "It is now. You have the right to know what it's all about." She laughed huskily. "It was about you in an indirect way. That's how it started, anyway, I think." She looked nervously away, covered her eyes with a hand.

"Oh?"

A long silence followed and suddenly Paul was aware of her shoulders shaking.

"What's wrong?" he asked foolishly.

She didn't turn; she didn't look at him. Her shoulders shook harder and then he heard soft choking sounds held-back sobs. Emotion welled in Paul and he put an arm around Lynn's shoulders.

"It's all right, Lynn," he said tenderly. "You don't

have to—"

"No! I have to!" she finally said, pushing gently away, wiping her eyes with the back of her hand like a little child.

"Please, Lynn."

"No!" she exploded almost angrily. "I have to tell you because I...just because...so you'll understand all about me!" She hesitated. "A cigarette?"

He lighted one for her and put it between her lips. She dragged deeply, then turned, looked out the window.

"I don't know what kind of woman you think I am—but regardless, Paul—regardless of what I'll tell you—I'm not a cheap tramp. I've told you I like sex—but not with everybody. I don't throw my body around...just... just like that!" Her voice choked to silence and then after a while started again. "Paul, Jack is a real bastard. You don't know. All I can tell you is that the first time...the first time...he...forced me—he did things—hit me...I was frightened because there wasn't anybody I could really turn to. It would have been too much of a laugh. Bryon doesn't give a damn, really! And...well, Jack did it that time...and after that—I was afraid—like you don't know how afraid I was! I hate his guts!" The last words spat out violently. "I'd kill him if I knew how to do it...safely!" She laughed almost bitterly at that. "I don't know how much I can stand...this...never again. I know that. I knew that the last time—after we, you and me, made love—I knew it couldn't happen again between Jack and me—not like that! Not him! Never!"

"Lynn...why torture yourself and—?"

"Please," she sighed in an emotional voice on the verge of tears, "let me finish."

She gasped in a deep breath and continued. "He came here, today, and wanted...well you can guess what he wanted. I tried, politely—as possible—to tell him that...well, I wasn't in the mood. I just finally came out and, said that...I didn't want to. He called me a little whore...and a few more names like that and I...well, slapped his face, and you must have seen the rest and—" She shrugged.

"I figured something like that," Paul said, inwardly furious at Jack Myers. "I didn't mean to sound—well, what I

43

said over the phone this afternoon—"

He felt suddenly cheap and sick inside.

Lynn offered, without excuses: "Oh, crap! Forget it. I was working on a hangover—and anyway, you were right! I'm kept! But not in the way you think—or for the same reasons you think. I'm Bryon's sister-in-law, by a quick Mexican marriage and a quicker Vegas divorce. Anyway, I get money from Bryon. Little brother was in some trouble and couldn't keep up with his weekly checks. It's a long, dull story. The fact is that I have something on Billy-boy—my ex-husband—and though I'm not doing anything like blackmail, I do get paid my weekly sum...offered to me for my silence.

"In any case—I help dear old Bryon. He keeps me in style and I do favors for him. It's a simple arrangement—if you know what I mean. It happened all...over time. First his damned brother had me sucked into believing something that simply wasn't possible. He's a brute. Anyway...strange how things happen in life. You start down one path and end up in a jungle to survive any way you can! And worst of all we all take the road of least resistance when it's offered...especially when it's paved with hard cash. You can understand all that, can't you?"

Paul didn't exactly know what to think, but said nothing about it.

They stood there for a long time without saying anything more and then Lynn broke the silence with:

"Well, anyway, Jack wanted me to play more bed games with him. Said that if I was so willing to shack up with you I should be willing to give a little to him, too. He called me all the dirty names, and I called him a few more inventive dirty names and he hit me. Thanks. Any time I can do you a favor, let me know."

Paul just shrugged and sat down on the sofa. A few minutes later Lynn settled next to him.

"Well, anyway, to what do I owe the pleasure of your visit? Surely not for the purpose of saving me from a fate worse than death."

They both laughed.

Lynn placed a gentle, warm hand on his thigh, press-

44

ing lightly. It was a sensual action that charged a sudden surge of desire through him. The implication was complete, without any need for talking about it. But for a moment Paul ignored the offer. He leaned back and then turned his eyes toward Lynn.

"You're quite a puzzling woman."

"How's that?" she murmured in a low, rich voice, her eyes sparkling.

"I don't know. Only that I—well, to be brutal about it, you don't seem to fit the role you're playing."

Silence answered him, but her face seemed to flicker with a soft glow of warmth.

"You know, Lynn, I could get to like you a lot. Don't ask me why. There have been enough women in my life—and to be truthful—"

"I'm a tramp, only a tramp, not worthy of 'liking,' is that it?" she completed, bitter sounding.

"I don't think I'd put it that way. Let's just say that neither of us is a particularly good catch. I'm a bum, who jumps from one thing to another. No real roots. Really directionless. I left high school and joined the Army, did my stint and then came home to just drift. And now I have drifted ... here."

He shrugged, self-consciously, uncertain what he had meant by that confession. "You've been making it the hard way. Yet, there's real feeling...here, between us. And that is crazy, 'cause we don't know one another. Don't ask me to explain, because I can't."

Lynn merely smiled, saying nothing.

They sat there for a long time, silently aware of one another.

Lynn broke the silence with: "Paul, I wasn't always like this."

"I know—you told me first time around."

"No! I didn't mean that. I mean that when I was younger—I came from a small town, with small-town moral attitudes. I was raised to believe that you made love only when you were in love—and you should be married, at that!"

"You don't have to explain; we're adult enough—"

"But I have to," she announced desperately, as if it

were very important to her.

She was silent for a moment then continued, after taking a deep drag on her cigarette. "In high school—in my last year—I met this man, and he said I had a talent for singing—and I was the only singer in school, and I had a pretty voice, but that's all you can say about it, really. He took a 'liking' to me. And offered me everything, like I told you before. He was staying with an aunt of his, and everything seemed 'all right', even to my folks. Well, as it worked out—we left town together. But everything was respectable. He was taking me to a big career in show business which ended on the couch and finally with his disappearance.

"It was my first experience and I really thought I was so much in love with him that he could do me no harm. Giving my body to him seemed only right. I thought we were to be married soon. Well, anyway, that made me pretty bitter. I went wild, I guess. I met Silvers' brother where I worked. I had fallen for the wrong kind of guy again. Anyway, that was short, and not so sweet."

Paul turned and looked at her. She wasn't the kind of woman to get serious with, yet he found himself wanting to understand her and forgive her for what she was. He wished, with all his heart, that things were different. "Look, Lynn, what you are today is all that matters. What you've been— done in the past—can be forgotten. The only thing that matters is that we managed to have fun together. I suppose. We shouldn't think about anything else."

She nodded, as if he'd expressed her very thoughts. "I liked you right from the beginning. I guess that's why we ended up here in the first place. For what that's worth..."

"It's worth a lot, Lynn. Everybody has to fight life the best they can—some are lucky—some aren't. Hell, if two adult people want to discover each other, why should they be bothering themselves with any other thoughts? The trouble with our society is that there's too much made of it all. We only live once and we're fools not to make the most of it. So—enough of that?"

He reached for her and she melted into his arms like an overgrown child. It was then that he guessed the tragic, startling truth: Lynn was falling in love with him. That

46

thought annoyed Paul; then he pushed it aside. Time would take care of everything.

* * * * * * *

The next two days were strangely wonderful. Paul stayed with Lynn, mostly sharing the bed in this prolonged escape into physical intimacy. They got up, dressed, only to go out and buy groceries. They were living in a world of make-believe, with no future and no past. Paul found a wonderful release and fulfillment in Lynn, a kind that he had never experienced with another woman. And in that way it was a startling and strange relationship. A tramp and a questionable bum. In a way he kept remembering what Gina had told him—yet oddly enough without any emotional or actual mental memory of what they had shared together—that she was a Mistress of the Damned. In a way, he realized, he was a Slave of the Damned, and Lynn a part of that damned dimension where only questionable people lived out questionable lives.

He found himself wanting never to return to reality, to never seek out the world beyond the walls of Lynn's apartment. It was as if this were a perfect escape from the trouble of existence. Life was difficult and moments like these, little islands of near fantasy with a person willing to share it with you were lovely make believe. Not reality; but a wonderful side-dimension to life, which only happened from time to time, when two people connected in a special way. Neither of them was making any demands; and held no expectations. But both of them were enjoying each other in a very important way—a shared daydream that held no logic beyond its own existence.

They had been sitting on the bed; Lynn snuggled close to him, when the phone rang.

The jarring sound of the phone was like an explosion cutting through them. Paul first to respond, almost angrily, irritably, hated himself, hating the world that was daring to intrude into their fantasy of escape.

"Ignore it!" he finally ordered, knowing at the same time how impossible it would be to do so.

47

Lynn slowly, eyes holding a strange sense of defeat, shook her head. "No, Paul, no. It has to end—now is as good a time as any."

Lynn stepped across the room, hesitated at the door-way, and then turned to face him. Her eyes were a study of pain, moist and shining. She blew him a kiss and then slipped into the other room. He heard her voice but didn't actually listen to the words. It wasn't until she called that Paul was jarred back to cruel reality.

Reluctantly Paul went into the living room. He slid an arm around Lynn's waist, kissing her neck with all emotion within him, fighting back the choking sensation that tightened his throat. Then he took the receiver and said: "Hello?"

"Silvers," a harsh voice crackled over the line. "We're ready for the second trip. Tonight, at two in the morning. Have the plane ready."

"Anything else?" Paul inquired, inwardly fighting a sickness that he didn't want to explain to himself.

The phone went dead and Paul replaced the receiver, looked at Lynn.

"It's over, isn't it, Paul?" Lynn said in a voice that was not really a question but more of a statement. Tears were beginning to creep down her wide cheeks.

"Hey, you don't do that!" he said in a tender voice, wiping the tears away from her beautiful face. "We've shared a wonderful experience, together. Reality? Well, that's a different story. But over? Maybe a fantasy always has to end. Anyway…a part of me simply adores you!"

"Oh, Paul," she murmured against his check, clinging to him. "That's such a nice thing to say."

"It's true, Lynn. Doesn't matter how long a relation-ship last, some happen and exist on their own, in their own place and time. Maybe…who knows? But I think you're really a nice person. I really mean that."

"You do?" The tears welled in her eyes.

"Now, none of that!" he teased her, gently wiping a tear off her cheek.

"I don't care—and I want to cry!" Lynn choked out. "It's been so wonderful, the two of us, these…hours to-

48

gether. Kinda…like magic. Wasn't it?"

"Very much so," he assured her, kissing those soft lips ever so tenderly. "Very much."

"And now…it's over...?"

"It doesn't have to be," he told her, fighting back the emotion which was welling to his own eyes He was hating himself for having any emotion, for there was no reason to have it.

"It's not the same. Maybe this was a moment we had, together. A really nice one. It could never be the same."

"Why should it be different?" he asked, knowing the answer already.

"No, Paul. You know it, too. It's going to be different!" She hid her face against his cheek, crying softly. For a long time they stood there silently.

Then she moved away, an embarrassed laugh on her lips. "That was silly as all hell, wasn't it?"

Paul merely shook his head. He didn't trust his voice any more. The hard lump in his throat was already beginning to tighten too much. He didn't want to leave their lovely island away from the world—and island made of a mutual desire to share these precious moments together. If only life were different; if only reality wasn't so cruel.

CHAPTER FIVE

It was late in the morning when they finally took to the air for Mexico. The sky was blood red, streaking the eastern sky. The air had been chilled before take-off and only several cups of hot coffee had taken the chill from Paul's bones. Conversation between Silvers and Myer had been casual, but general in nature as the three of them awaited take-off. Other men had been kept busy loading the plane with crates, which were to be shipped to Mexico. Myer made no effort to be pleasant to Paul, and Silvers, being the boss, seemed to see no reason to make any effort to carry on a conversation with his hired pilot. As far as the two men had been concerned, Paul was a "thing" to be ignored. At least for the most part.

Paul had smoked half a pack of cigarettes and watched the two passengers he was hired to fly to Mexico—and he watched the cargo being loaded. A sense of depression ate at him—the kind of depression that was hard to identify. He thought of Lynn Palmer many times and remembered the sweet beauty of her body, the scent of her as he had held her close. The image of Lynn was like a haunting ghost that he couldn't escape from.

When Paul saw Silvers motioning that it was time to leave, he was glad to get his mind on other matters. The plane's compartment had been loaded with huge boxes of ammunitions, guns, and explosives

Silvers and Myer sat in the back there in silence, waiting out the long flight.

Paul was alone in the cockpit, deep in his own thoughts again, grabbed by his own doubts about life. Concerned about this job. And once again his mental wandering

returned to Lynn. But that wasn't until he was already high
in the sky, mechanically guiding the plane toward its destination. He once more thought of the passion and the affection
which Lynn inspired in him. It was amazing how close they
had been and their last few moments together had rammed
home a very hard fact: this woman was very special—in a
strange way. A meaningful fantasy of what might be in another universe where harsh reality didn't exist made only of
lovely dreams.

Finally the trip came to an end, and he slowly settled
the plane down upon the long strip of sandy beach that was
surrounded by water and hot, thick tropical jungle.

They were met, as before, by a group of men who
had that seedy appearance of gangsters, Latin-style. They
began to empty the plane, placing the large heavy boxes on
the back of a pickup truck, parked nearby on the beach. A
man got behind the wheel and then drove down the beach.

Paul followed Silvers, Myer and their host, Santez,
along the pathway that led to the large bungalow. His mind
was occupied with thoughts of Lynn again. With that came a
frustration, for he simply didn't know what to make of her or
the feelings that she created in him.

*Wish we could get away from everything...just the
two of us.*

His fists clutched.

"You're being stupid!" he muttered to himself. *Forget Lynn!*

By the time they reached their host's house he was
desperately longing for some thing to clear his mind. Maybe
just get drunk. When he stepped into the living room behind
Jack Myer, an excited feminine voice called out happily.

"Paul!"

Instantly he recognized that voice and looked anxiously for the woman to whom it belonged. Almost immediately he spotted Gina standing only a few feet away.

She was dressed magnificently, in a tight-fitting yel-
low blouse, which accentuated the large thrust of her soft
breasts, and a flaring red skirt that hugged her waist and hips.
Her smile was seductive and inviting, leaving nothing to the
imagination. It was Latin heat, reaching out to him, embrac-

ing his body, and screaming to be burned to a blazing fire.

Myer, Silvers and Santez disappeared into another room without so much as a glance in his direction. Again, with that attitude that he didn't exist as far as they were concerned.

Screw them, he thought. *While I...do the same to Gina. But with a lovely difference. Damn right, that!*

He tried to focus his thoughts on nothing more.

Paul simply let himself devour her whole form. He was delighted to find her so willing to be with him. Maybe what he needed so desperately. It was as if he were looking at all-consuming fire.

Even so, there was a part of him that didn't want to be with any woman other than Lynn. And that's exactly what he needed to escape. And Gina was impossible to ignore. An invitation for a long night of being exhaustively drained by her fiery body.

She directed him into the kitchen, without a word. The flow of her body, moving in front of him, was simply a sensual dance, a seductive invitation, just so naturally announcing itself with every step.

"We have some food...what do you call them? Enchiladas...yes? And tacos? Yes?"

"Yes. We have a lot of Mexican places in the southwest."

"Yes. I thought so. Here, let me give you some of this."

She picked up a corn tortilla, found some beans and chucks of meat in deep red salsa. "Like it hot or mild?"

"You know I like it very hot!" he grinned, and her eyes flashed in response.

"Yes, I remember. You...what was it, called me hot...a hot tamale, I think. I thought you were the tamale, though. Very hot and delicious." She came close, extending a tortilla rolled skillfully around a slice of meat in red sauce. "This isn't too hot, I promise."

She lifted it to his mouth.

"Not as hot as me, anyway," she smiled and he took a bite.

She wiped some sauce from his lips and then she

53

licked her fingers, making it all look almost degenerately sexual. "I just think we do it good...you and me! That was some fun. Don't you think?"

She placed the rest of the rolled tortilla in his hand, patted his cheek. "Oh, you are hot, flushed. Did I do that to you?"

He grinned, sat down at a small table, where she fixed a plate of food and then presented it to him. "You eat food, first. Then...I'm all yours! Yes?"

His eyes shot over her body, remembering the raw, animal pleasure that it had given him. Even if that was all she had to offer, nothing more vital, it might just be enough. Just want he needed. One hot tamale. And that might be what he needed.

She came on so seductively and in such a brazenly natural manner that there was no escape, even if he wanted to.

He ate in silence, while she watched him from across the table. Those eyes were intimate promises as they watched his every move.

"I was hoping," she said, smiling, taking a puff from the cigarette in her large lips, "you'd return."

"I thought you would know I'd be back," he countered, his voice level.

She laughed, a strangely harsh sounding laugh, then nodded, "Yes—but...I think you're nice. What'd you say? Hot! All over!"

Her eyes moved downwards, as if seeing through the table where his hips would be, silently saying *this is what I've been waiting for!*

"And what is the point?" he asked really to himself, hardly aware of having verbalized the thought. Without any question his body wanted her, responded to her, yet it wasn't this woman he really wanted to be with.

"Does there have to be a...point? You're nice, Paul!" Gina told him. "And, you kept out of trouble. With me. I kept you busy. They can do what they do. No worry about you not knowing what to do. I'm your entertainment! I told you that the other day—did you forget, already?"

"Guess the hired help are being tossed together," Paul

laughed, bitterly.

"Is that bad?" she wondered, softly. "Not bad. Nice. Good. I think. I like it with a man like you. Strong. Hard muscles. Women like hard men."

She smiled as if that line had some private, secret meaning all its own to her. It probably did.

He wondered what was going on in the other room that had to be kept so private—silenced from him. He felt the sense of uneasiness again, that uneasiness that this was not all it seemed to be—that, something was taking place which might go very much against his grain. But that was obviously silly. He had been hired to pilot his plane—nothing more.

"Well, Paul, what'd you think. About us?" Gina inquired, standing as he finished his meal. She placed her hands on her hips, challenging him with her large brown eyes. "Want to be...?"

"Let's go for a walk, okay?"

She looked momentarily disappointed, then finally nodded. "Why not? Who knows what might happen on a...walk. Where to?"

"The beach?"

"Oh. That can be fun, too!"

Paul could hardly keep from smiling at the reaction that lighted Gina's face. She didn't say anything about it, but obviously her thoughts were centered the idea of sex on the beach.

Paul thought he could question Gina. Maybe he would learn something about the little conference, find out what was so mysterious about it, and what it was that had to be kept so hushed up. He didn't expect her to tell him anything she wasn't supposed to, but a subtle hint might be all he needed to fill in the details.

He stood and she stepped in close, taking his hand in hers. A moment later they moved out through the living room and the outside.

Gina was letting no opportunity slip by to impress on him what she had in mind. Her hips brushed his as they stepped onto the porch in a sliding, highly sensual motion, as she made every effort to focus his mind on what she was offering, soon. Then they started silently to walk toward the beach.

He inquired where she'd learned to speak English so well.

"Men. And books. And I work hard. I dream. Someday, somehow, I get to the U.S.A. I become an American Citizen. I want to live there," she confessed. "I dream what it must be like. Live rich. Not poor like here. I come from small village."

He felt sorry for her, realizing how impossible that could be. A dream, though, which he didn't have the heart to squash.

Then she impulsively turned towards him. "I wish you could take me there?"

He merely smiled, and when she came into his arms there was no need to speak. She was soft and warm and her lips parted under his in a deeply passionate kiss. Instinctively his hands found her breasts, so soft and free under the blouse.

"You like?" she asked when the kiss broke.

"I like," he admitted, wanting to ravish her right there.

"I like, too," she admitted, touching his thigh. "I like you a lot, Mr. USA!"

"Hey, I'm not—"

"You are big man, strong. Makes a woman all ... what's the word?"

"What word?"

"Makes me want…that." She looked down pointedly at his groin. "Makes me…hot for it. That's the word. Right?"

She smiled so brightly that he found her delightfully charming. Appealing. And so bloody sexy.

"You make a man feel the same way, baby."

"We do it? Right. Right here? Or in my room? We do it here and there! Okay?"

She grabbed his hands and slipped them under her blouse, and up against her naked breasts.

"I like your hands. You feel good." She squeezed his fingers and her breasts surged up against them, warm and soft. "Here, we do it. Right?"

He was instantly dizzy with uncontrolled desire to totally smother himself against her body, to become completely enveloped within the woman's embrace. In moments she had lifted her blouse off and pulled his head down to her. After that all he knew was the joyful sensation of her hot flesh quickly responding to his uncontrolled kisses. That first time on the beach was so fast that he hardly realized what was happening. No waiting, no lingering, no wasted movement. They simply surged together in a wild ecstatic ride that didn't stop even once satisfied for the moment.

It seemed like hours had passed before Paul finally awoke to find Gina next to him on the sand. He felt a flutter of coldness shoot through him and wasn't sure if it was caused by the breeze which was slowly chilling or something else, less physical.

He looked at Gina and tried to tell himself that no matter what they had shared together, he must learn as much as possible from her. Why this seemed important he really didn't know. Yet, even though he felt nothing for the woman emotionally, there was the element of intimacy, which grows between man and woman when they have shared each other's bodies.

"Gina," Paul finally said, determined to come directly to the point, without any subtle buildups. She had earned that much honesty.

"Yes, Paul?" she said softly, looking up into his eyes, smiling. She slipped closer, sliding her arms around his neck, a contented expression in her eyes. Tenderness radiating from her like waves from an ocean. "Anything, Paul. Anything at all."

"You don't even know what I'm going to ask!" he cried, much too loud.

"Anything, Paul. Anything you ask, Paul!" she murmured, kissing his nose, caressing the back of his neck. The wind played with her short black hair, brushing it against his cheek. "Anything at all."

Paul was surprised by her words, her actions. They told him quite clearly that Gina was more than just fond of him. That she might love him was quite out of the question—but there was some kind of deep affection in her eyes. It didn't make sense, but that wasn't important; some times such things happened.

"What kind of revolution is Santez involved in?" Paul was startled by his own bold question, because he wasn't quite sure what he wanted to know—or how he had planned on going about finding out.

She sat there, next to him, looking into his eyes like a little child. But the expression on her face slowly darkened.

"Why you ask?" Gina finally questioned in a dull, lifeless voice.

"I don't know. Just interested, I guess. Curious, maybe." He lowered his eyes.

Gina was hugging herself suddenly to him.

"Does it matter?" she finally asked, pulling slightly away. "Does it really matter to you?"

"No, not really, I guess," he lied.

"Then why I should tell you!" She giggled, then kissed his ear. A moment later she reached for his hand and pressed it into the hot warmth of her breast.

It was this action, this evasion that sparked the next statement that again welled up from his subconscious, without hesitation, rather from his conscious mind. It surprised Paul as much as it did the woman.

"It's one of those local revolts, isn't it?" he demanded, something going cold inside. He hated politics. And the Latin American countries were continually finding reasons to over-throw the present corrupt government by replacing it with another corrupt gang of thieves. It seemed so purposeless. And other people, like this woman, were caught in that web without any escape. No wonder they wanted to come to America.

Gina tensed, her body freezing hard against his. It was all the answer he needed. That silence was enough to tell even a fool that he'd hit a raw nerve.

A cold nausea flushed through Paul, a tight clamping hand squeezed his throat dry, turned his stomach inside out. Again he'd gotten himself involved with the one element in the world he wanted to avoid like a rotting sickness of the grave.

What now, little man? He wondered, fighting hard to control the emotions about to expose his true feelings. Then

58

other thoughts plagued him.

Was Silvers a commie? Or did that term mean anything any more? Most of the liberators were either that or linked with some terrorist movement. It was political or religious or just power plays between gangster types. The world was coming apart and there was little any one person could do about that. The poor wanted some of the riches, and the rich wanted to keep it all for themselves. And just about everybody else was caught in between, unable to get out of that trap—and certainly unable to change things.

Or did Silvers just support terrorist movements? Or was he merely a businessman dealing in whatever properties that brought in big bucks?

Was Lynn politically involved?

That last stung. Deep.

Suddenly Paul felt terribly alone, trapped in a world in which he wanted no part—but from which there was no escape. It was the kind of loneliness that a man feels only a few times in his life—the kind that eats terribly through every nerve and makes him want to cry like a baby, lost.

Paul immediately found himself not wanting to think about anything. Especially about Lynn and the very good possibility that she might be involved in this game, too, very personally. After all, he knew next to nothing about her.

There was only one escape for him—and that was Gina—the mistress of the damned.

She literally dragged him to her, thighs parting in wild open invitation as their lips met. "Oh...! She moaned, hugging his head in her hand. "Yes...!" She murmured a few moments later, urging him down to her breasts, moving him from one to the other, until he felt her fingers clinging tighter at the back of his head.

"Oh, Paul," she murmured, pressing him down further. "Kiss me..."

And the blunt meaning of her plea was blatantly obvious as her hips literally arched towards him. After that he was simply smothered in the heat of the woman who wouldn't let him go until they were both exhausted beyond moving. How long they lay there in the sand, he didn't know. The surf breaking in the background brought slow

consciousness back into place and he remembered everything.

He stood, looking down at the woman's naked body,
lying on her back. Her eyes met his, her lips parted in a generous warm smile.

"I dreamed...you took me to America, in your
plane."

He smiled at her, shrugged. "Well, we all dream."

"I wish it could be...going there ... being an American Citizen."

"I suppose so. A dream, of course."

"It could happen. Maybe happen."

He didn't know exactly what to say to that, but
merely kissed her forehead. "I suppose life is hard for you
here."

"Not so hard. He takes good care. I have to...well, do
what he wants. But...someday maybe I get to America.
Maybe it happen."

He tried to avoid the subject. "I like you. A lot of
fun." He cupped her breast, ever so gently. "Really like
you."

"Oh, Paul, you're so good to Gina!" She reached up
for him. "We are good together. No? Would be nice if we
run away together. Right? Maybe you take me to USA?
How'd that be? We could be together...like this?"

"Sure. I don't think so, not that easy."

"Why not? You have a plane."

"Not that simple."

She frowned, then shrugged. "Well, I like being with
you. We were good!"

"You've done me in," he managed.

The look in her eyes, and the way they literally
flowed over him, seem to suggest she didn't believe a word
he had just said.

Paul didn't care. But he gently reached out and when
she was standing, said: "Better that we get back, now." Both
of them stood and moved quickly to her quarters to continue
lingering on what had just transpired between them.

Paul was glad when they returned to the bungalow.
The feeling of deep depression broke over him as he sat

alone in the living room. Gina had cheerfully said she needed to do something and left him. She hadn't dressed, though he had.

The idea of supplying arms and aid to the Communists, revolutionist or terrorist was not only against his own personal convictions, but also against the laws of the United States.

He realized how right Lynn Palmer had been when she had warned him about Silvers.

But too late.

Now all the man would have to do was point out that he had helped to supply a people with arms for revolt in a Latin American country—and that would be enough to keep any normal guy in line. Right under the man's thumb!

A nervous tug snapped at his guts, as if a spring had suddenly broken and twisted around it. What could he, a lone, unarmed man, do against a group of desperate people like this? The thought was stunning, frightening. Up to that moment he'd never actually considered doing anything against these men. After all, money was money. If he didn't do the job, somebody else would. That was, at least in part, some of his rationale for signing up even for this one job. But now he felt totally different about everything. He had to do something. But what?

How long he sat there it was impossible to know, for sure. He was convinced it was over an hour.

When Jack Myer and Bryon Silvers stepped into the living room, it was a little past 9 p.m. and Paul wondered, vaguely, where Gina was, but put the thought immediately out of his mind. The less he thought about women right then the better it would be for him. He stood, trying to appear casual.

"Where to?" he asked, looking at Silvers.

"You'll be told when to jump, fly-boy," Myer sneered nastily. "When we get around to telling you!" Then, as an afterthought, he dug deep with a finishing remark: "Why don't you go to your little whore, Gina? That's what she's here for, keeping pricks like you out of trouble. And keeping them from asking too many questions they have no business asking! Keeping little boys busy!"

61

Paul frowned, holding back the anger that shot through him.

Silvers, sensing the obviously dangerous tension between the two of them, stepped forward, patted Paul's shoulder "We'll be leaving tomorrow. Santez is having a meal prepared. After that, we'll retire. Okay?"

Paul felt the depressive grind of hate slowly weigh down heavily upon him once more.

Silvers continued in a silky voice, "Oh, by the way, if you'd like to make a little more money, Paul, I'll be needing you to make some more shipments to Mr. Santez here."

Paul tried to hold down the sudden fear that ate at him. "What if I can't?"

Silvers grinned and exchanged knowing looks with Jack Myer. Paul didn't miss the meaning behind the man's silence.

Silvers turned again to face Paul. "Maybe if I were to throw in a thousand more for each trip would you be able to do me that favor?" There was hardness in the man's gray eyes, threatening and dangerous. His lips clamped around the thick cigar like some kind of iron trap.

"No arguments," Paul assured him, attempting to smile. There was no reason to complicate matters. What happened later, once back in the states, might be another matter. Until then, it was better for him to simply play along. "Suits me fine."

Already, he was making plans. Somehow he had to turn the situation around in some way, to bring an end to all of this. But how? His mind raced over every possibility. Nothing felt right. Finally he settled on the only sane thing which would make sense to work: once back in the States, he would inform the FBI. It was their problem, not his. They had methods that would work—he might end up dead if he tried anything on his own.

They had a couple of cocktails before dinner, which killed about thirty minutes. The dinner was served in a huge dining room which had a large table centered in it. Thin juicy steaks, done Mexican style. Beans and tortillas. The conversation was light and general, never hinting upon the true activities that these men were involved in. It was difficult to think about Santez as being anything but an intelligent, respectable Latin American host. He was cultured and refined.

After dinner, several more drinks were passed. Paul thought of finding Gina to spend the night with, then decided against it. He allowed himself to be given a room. To his surprise, he it shared with Jack Myer.

For the first time, he tried to break through the iron hatred that had wedged itself between them. Paul reasoned that it might be possible to learn something from the other guy. When they were alone in the room he turned to Myer, saying as pleasantly as possible: "Look, Jack, we've been riding each other's back right from the first day. There's no reason we can't get along...how about it?"

With that, Paul extended his hand, and fought the grinding sensation at the pit of his stomach at touching the other man.

Myer looked up at him in disgust. "What's with you, fly-boy. Losing your nerve?"

"What? How's that?"

"Nothing. Just forget it. We have a score to settle—if you'll remember. And it'll be my pleasure when I get my chance. That's one thing I'm looking forward to, anxiously!" His eyes filled with hatred. Slowly he began undressing.

"Look, Jack, I'm sorry about the other day." Paul found himself sickened by these words, but it was the only way possible that he might get through to the man. But even as he spoke, it was obvious it had been a waste.

"You'll be sorry, fly-boy. Real sorry, all right. So will Lynn!" the man threatened.

Paul tensed, as if slapped, his eyes growing hot. "You leave her out of this!"

Jack Myer laughed, pulling his undershirt off, revealing heavy broad chest muscles, thick hairy arms. Paul was amazed that he had managed to overpower this man. Myer was a mountain of steel muscles.

"Don't try anything with Lynn!" Paul warned again, not revealing the sudden raw fear that knifed at his gut.

The man ignored him, going into the small bathroom, slamming the door.

Paul wondered why the two of them had been

roomed together and also wondered if Jack Myer had arranged it that way. He reconsidered his ideas about not being with Gina. Her soft, warm body was far more appealing than being anywhere near Jack Myer.

He walked to the door and started to step out into the hall, then hesitated, turned and went back into the room. Running out might do a lot of damage. Myer was probably holding off because of an instinctive fear of the cowardly bastard he so obviously was. If he thought Paul was afraid, running out of an awkward situation, his hate might just break out into open violence. Paul shuddered at the thought of having a real run-in with Jack Myer. It would be necessary to be on the alert from now on.

That one encounter which had favored Paul against Myer, was possibly just a lucky first punch break. The other man hadn't been prepared for Paul's assault. Next time it would be quite different. Even man to man the balance of power might lean in Myer's direction. Chances were, the man would bring in some of his friends to assure in total dominance.

All Paul had to do was keep things at arms distance. All Paul needed was time to inform the Federal Government about Silvers. Time might play into his hands, for surely it would only be a matter of days before this whole mess would be settled.

Shrugging, Paul undressed. He looked forward to a long, restless night.

CHAPTER SIX

The next morning, a rough hand shaking his shoulder awakened Paul. His eyes shot open, and he looked slowly up, finding Jack Myer standing over him like some mountain of muscles. Those dark eyes were angry, seething—and if a look could kill, Paul Phillips would have been dead at that moment.

"Fly-boy—time to get on the ball. We leave!" The man's tone of voice was demanding and insulting.

Paul lay there for several moments trying to collect his thoughts. The dry, pasty texture of his mouth mixed with the hammering at his temples revealed he had boozed it up a little too much the evening before.

Slowly he slid out of bed, doing his best to ignore the other man.

Several hours later Jack Myer, Silvers and Paul were in flight over Mexico, on their way back to the States. For Paul, the long trip was a study of anxiety. He was all too painfully aware of the problem that faced him. His mind was frantically trying to work out a way of explaining to the FBI about Silvers, without placing himself in any immediate danger. He didn't like the idea of babbling to the police like a little snot-nosed kid; but there wasn't really anything else he could do that was sane.

When they arrived in Los Angeles it was early afternoon, the sun hot in the sky, bright and almost blinding.

Myer and Silvers were first to leave the airfield. Paul waited until the other two men had gone before going to his car. He had managed to make himself look busy enough by tinkering with the plane. When he finally sat in his car, he lighted a cigarette and tried, once more, to sort out his thoughts. Tried, once more, to decide what he had to do next—what the most safe, intelligent move might be.

It was several minutes before Paul realized the cause of his nervousness and immediate hesitation.

Lynn Palmer. How involved had she become in this nasty web? Was she part of it? Lynn Palmer might be more involved than he had thought. That story about being Silvers' ex-sister-in-law wasn't exactly phony, but it certainly was up for grabs. And what did she really know about Silvers' actual activities?

He didn't want to be responsible for doing anything that might hurt Lynn more than life seemed to already have done. Lynn had enough trouble already. He didn't think the woman needed any more. On the other hand, Paul forced himself to admit, if she were a Communist, or consciously working for the Communists, then it was his duty to stop her.

Paul finally decided he had to see Lynn, find out as much as possible, before doing anything that might involve an innocent party Or, if she were merely trapped—find a way to pull her free from the trap before it crushed her

But instead of going directly to Lynn's apartment, he drove to his place, showered, changed, and had several strong shots of whiskey to sooth the nerves straining within him. Later, he found himself sitting nervously in the small living room, brooding over the problem again, not wanting to face the truth, not wanting, really, to do anything but sit by and let things happen...without getting himself in the way.

Then, at last, Paul realized that he was merely making excuses for not taking any action. This depressed and confused him more. He had a lot of thinking to do before taking any first gigantic step which could shove him down into a pit of hellish death—anything might go wrong. Did he want to risk his life? Did he want to become that involved? It was one thing to die for your country—another to simply toss your life away for nothing.

* * * * * * *

Lynn was just coming into her apartment, after doing a little window shopping, when a hand reached out and shoved her brutally into the room, knocking her against the door. Her first shocked, frightened awareness cut away all other thoughts.

"What the hell?" she cried, trying to understand what had just happened.

The door slammed shut behind her.

Then, just as suddenly as fear had choked at her, Lynn recovered slightly. She twisted around, fighting mad, and found herself face to face with a leering Jack Myer. The expression on the man's face knifed the terror back through Lynn even stronger than before. His eyes, dark, dangerous, were large and violent, as if some seething anger were bubbling there and about to explode.

Instinctively Lynn looked for some place to run and hide. But, of course, there was no escape from this man—not here. She realized that, all too quickly and felt suddenly so alone, so isolated from the world.

The man jerked forward reaching for her, like a snake snapping out for attack. Lynn attempted to avoid him.

"Jack—what's wrong?" she breathed out between tense white lips.

"Slut! Shut up, slut!" Without warning his right hand lashed out, striking her face in a brutal blow which jarred through her whole frame. Then Lynn felt herself being grabbed by large, cruel hands, digging deep into her shoulders, hurting. It was like a terrible nightmare. She struggled as the man attempted to pull her into his arms, his lips large, wide, and passionate in their demand to find her mouth. His pure brute strength was too much for any woman.

"Please, Jack, don't..."

But the man's lips muffled her outcry, moist, greedy.

His hand struck her face once more. His slanderous contempt continued: "You're getting just a sample of what's coming, bitch. I've had it with you, for good!"

He stood there leering, his eyes suddenly burning bright

"Jack you don't have to do it this way," Lynn breathed, backing from the man, realizing there was no escape from him.

He stood there, laughing at her. And then something

happened so unexpectedly, so unreasonably, that Lynn could hardly believe it.

Jack's fist reached out like a sledgehammer, slamming into her face, knocking her half way across the room. She staggered under the terrible impact of the blow. She stumbled, fell, hitting her head against the hard floor. Stunned, dazed, Lynn lay there helplessly for several moments, unable to believe this was really happening to her. Then Myer was on her, jerking at her bra until it came away, hurting the tender flesh.

She screamed a muffled scream, terror taking volume from her yell of fear.

What happened after that was more than a nightmare, because it was a reality that could not be escaped. The man took her physically, pinning her body, ramming himself deep into her like a horrid steel pipe. She tried to cut her mind away from what was happening, attempting to blank it out.

Lynn wanted, with all her heart, to scream. It all seemed too savagely horrible, because she couldn't understand why it was happening to her. Then she was aware of what the man was doing to her in a crude animal way. His lips were greedy, his hands harsh, cruel, hurting with a savage happy lust.

If only Paul were there. But she was alone to face this horror and alone, she would have to face it—or sanity would run wild, leave forever. With that thought, Lynn realized that she was fighting for more than her body, her pain, her emotions, for her sanity.

Lynn now was fighting on two fronts, a physical and a mental one. All she wanted to do was hide in a dark corner, away from this hungry man's eyes, and cry. Forever cry.

Lynn knew why it was so impossible to want another man, even in her thoughts. It was because she was desperately in love with Paul. That really didn't make sense, considering how short a time they had known one another. Yet instinctively she did know. And that was final.

Then she heard Jack Myer's voice coming through the dazed red mist before her eyes.

"...That's just a sample, baby. That's payment for the fly-boy. He'll get his...when the time comes. You keep away from him! Understand? Of course you understand. Or I'll fix you up so that you don't look at another man—because no man will look at you! I'll fix that beautiful face of yours for good!"

She heard his footsteps and then the front door opened and slammed shut, the sound ringing throughout the room like thunder and shattering her ears.

Lynn lay there bathed in her anguish, shaking, tears streaming down her face. She lay there for a long time, weak, exhausted—so sick inside. It was a long time before she was actually able to comprehend the threat Jack Myer had made about Paul. His last remarks had been all too obvious in their meaning.

She didn't care about calling for help; not the kind that would really bring an end to the nightmare. And even that kind of out-reach would probably get her nowhere but deeper into trouble. It would only put Paul into a more critical danger zone from which he couldn't possibly escape. That was the double-bind she found herself in. And because of that, she was alone. But that had been the deal right from the beginning. This was something she'd have to resolve on her own, without any help. It was impossible for her to act without warning Paul and without finding out exactly how he stood on this whole bloody mess.

Slowly her reserve strength straightened her shoulders, fought down the horror that was engulfing her, emotionally. She started for the front door. She had to find Paul. She had to warn him.

* * * * * * *

Paul was still sitting in his apartment. It was impossible to know, for sure, how many hours had passed; it felt like he had been sitting there for an eternity. He was still helpless in his struggle to overcome the fears and the hesitation that plagued his mind.

It was around eight in the evening when the front doorbell rang. That sound jarred his ears, like knives. He hadn't realized how relaxed his body was, how deep in the mental pit of confusion his thoughts had drifted.

Paul sat up, startled. He put his half-empty glass on the stand next to the chair, in which he had been sitting and then slowly went to the door and opened it.

He slammed back like a man who has been hit by a fist. Even if his mind had been functioning properly he could have never guessed who would be standing there.

Recovering, Paul moved forward, helping Lynn into the room, quickly closing the door behind her.

She collapsed in his arms, sobbing like a child, her whole body shaking violently.

Paul felt sick at the sight of Lynn's face, bruised and caked with streaks of blood.

"Where is he?" he demanded, immediately guessing whom it was that had done this to her. He guided her across the room to the sofa.

"Where is Myer?" he cried between clinched teeth.

"I don't know," Lynn told him in a distorted shaky voice. "I just don't know!"

"Monster!" Paul cursed, his fists balling up at his side, his eyes narrowing.

Lynn shook her head slowly. "I...I hoped you'd be here...safe! I was terrified—scared he'd gotten to you and..."

"When'd it happen?" Paul wanted to know, shooting the question at her like a bullet.

"A little while ago. I—I came home—and he was there—afterwards—I came here—as soon as I could!" Her words had exhausted her. She looked up at him, pleadingly.

"You'll be okay!" he told her gently.

"Jack told me that this was a—warning...and for—something about you—something you'd done to him. Because of me—I think. I can't remember everything. It's a nightmare...God!" She covered her face with trembling hands and for a moment sobbed.

Paul put a tender arm around her shoulder.

Finally Lynn gained control of her voice. "He said he'd get around to you and—"

"I'm calling the police!" Paul announced, starting for the phone. "I'll get a doctor, too."

Lynn tensed, shaking her head. The expression on her face stopped him.

"No—Paul. Don't!"

He hesitated, uncertain what to do.

"Jack said if I went to the police he'd kill me—and you!" Lynn announced.

Paul's mouth dropped, surprised.

"That's the oldest bluff in the world. He wouldn't dare!"

Lynn laughed. It was a harsh, bitter sound. "How innocent can you get?" she asked. "Just take my word for it, Paul. He can—and he will kill us, if he wants to!"

"The police will have him behind bars so fast he won't know what happened to him!" Paul announced; realizing how foolish that sounded. He reached for the phone, lifting the receiver.

"No! Stop!" Lynn screamed.

Paul turned, startled, unable to believe the desperation in her voice.

"You don't know what you're doing, Paul!" she said, more quietly, now. "These guys play rough. They aren't playing games. Even if Jack Myer didn't kill us—Silvers would!" She hesitated, then added: "Don't you know what would happen? Don't you know what kind of people we're involved with?"

Paul was almost afraid to hear anymore; but she said it before he could stop her.

"They're worse than Communists used to be! More like terrorist. Only they don't have any morality! No ethics. No convictions other than their personal gain. It is money, power. And with Jack, well, he's crazy. But they fight to win."

Paul found his mind icing over. A terrible chill formed down his spine as he looked at the beautiful woman sitting before him.

It wasn't until she had spoken those last words that he realized his feeling for her had been so strong, so powerful. And he didn't like that, because he didn't want to care.

"Where does that put you and me?" he finally questioned.

She looked at him, puzzled for a long time. Her breathing was suddenly hard.

"That depends," she finally said in a level, controlled voice. "What are you going to do about it now, Paul?"

"Why?" Paul managed to choke out, pleading for her to tell him that she really wasn't truly personally involved. He wanted to hear this woman tell him that she didn't want anything to do with Silvers. Desperately he wanted to hear the right words from her.

But Lynn merely shook her head from side to side.

Paul sighed, determined, "You know what I'll have to do, don't you?"

Lynn's eyes snapped to his, wide, and there was a brightness to them, which surprised Paul. Almost hope.

"What?" she demanded, as if it was more important than anything in the world to know what he was actually going to do.

Paul hated himself for what he was about to do, but there was no possible escape. No possible turning aside any longer.

"I don't want anything to do with this setup, Lynn. Nothing! You said they could get a strong hold on me and I couldn't get out. Well, I'm getting out in the only possible way I can.

"If only things were different. If only I didn't care about you, Lynn!"

She started to say something, but Paul cut her short with a chop of his hand, cutting the air in front of him.

"No! I realize it's nuts! But I can't help myself. I'd give anything—anything at all if you'd tell me you weren't involved. But, I..." He shrugged helplessly.

"I have to do what's necessary," he told her, suddenly sick inside at himself and at the world, and at the trap that life had made for him—and for Lynn.

Lynn suddenly stood, rushing into his arms, before he was able to do anything.

Her lips breathed into his ear: "Oh, thank God, thank God. Thank God, Paul!"

She sobbed like a child.

Paul gently pushed her at arms' distance, stared into her eyes, unbelievingly. "Don't you know what I'm telling you?"

72

She happily shook her head, tears running down her smooth creamy cheeks.

"I have to inform on you and..." he started to say, but she interrupted him with a shake of her head.

"I'll give you a number to call. I had to find out about you...to make sure, before I could make my own move—report. I wanted to know how involved you were. How you felt about all this." The words flooded out, at first holding no meaning.

Slowly as Paul stood there staring at her, the meaning of what she had said started to suggest itself to him. It seemed too impossible. Then he found himself saying: "You're not making sense!"

Lynn smiled, more calmly now, more unemotionally, explained: "I found out about their little activities from my ex-husband. I reported to the FBI and they had me keep working with Silvers."

She laughed with happiness. "Anyway—call the number and tell the man where you are, what your name is and give my name. They'll do the rest. You'll be given instructions and—well, we'll see what happens then. Okay?"

"I don't get it," Paul exploded, still dazed.

"Don't try. I tried to warn you at the beginning—the only way I could do so. Anyway, Silvers isn't a Communist in the strict sense of the word. He just deals with them, terrorists, anybody political or...he doesn't care just so they have the hard cash. A real no-good gummy bastard!"

Paul continued to stare at Lynn, still unable to believe what he was hearing.

She wasn't any less a tramp, but she was one with a lot more character than anybody might have imagined. She had a hard, loyal sense of morality.

Lynn gave him a number to call.

Paul felt a sense of excitement as he started dialing. For once in his life he was doing something which had immediate meaning, a purpose and there was a real woman who actually meant something to him in a big way!

Just as the number started ringing there was a brutal, harsh knocking on the door. Paul tensed. He looked at Lynn, then at the door, and back to Lynn. Her eyes were large, wide, frightened, as if she were expecting the worst. Paul hesitated, not knowing what to do. Then the knocking grew louder, more demanding. After a moment, shrugging, Paul replaced the receiver on the hook and moved to the door.

"Who is it?" he asked.

"Myer. Let me in, Paul!"

The sound of the voice was so light and pleasant that it disarmed Paul. Without hesitation he swung the door open. No sooner had he opened the door than Myer smashed out an iron fist to the point of Paul's jaw.

Paul staggered backwards under the force of the blow, stunned, unable to adjust to the sudden attack. He sank to the floor, the world spinning around his head like black fog.

As he started for his feet, fighting his way through the red mist and blackness that was swimming around him, Paul found himself suddenly staring into the black point of a cold and deadly .38 revolver.

The door slammed loudly shut behind Jack Myer, who was now leering at him, a grin twisting his fat features.

"What's the meaning of this?" Paul managed, playing the innocent.

Jack laughed a cruel, huge, ugly laugh. And then he motioned with the gun.

"Sit next to your little whoring tramp! And be careful the way you move."

"You wouldn't use that. Not here in the middle of the city. Somebody would hear," Paul pointed out.

"Try me, just try me!" Myer rasped.

Lynn grabbed Paul's shoulder, cried: "He means it, Paul. Do what he says, for God's sake—and mine!"

Paul hesitated and then slipped closer to Lynn. He held her trembling hand in his.

"Aren't you a pretty pair? Just lucky I followed Lynn. I heard what went on in here. Silvers will be interested, quite interested. You can believe me!" Myer walked to the phone, dialed, waited. His eyes kept flickering toward Paul, never once giving him a chance to make a mad rush.

"Bryon. Jack. I'm at the fly-boy's place. Trouble. Lynn's here, too." He hesitated, then said: "They're a couple of double-dealing bastards. Yes. Lynn's been working with the Feds." He was silent for a while; his lips grinned wider and wider, revealing a terrible perverse pleasure at what he was hearing. "Yes, sir! Can do! I'll meet you there!"

Myer slammed the phone down on the hook and then jerked toward Paul and Lynn. His lips sneered into a distorted grin. "Well, it's back to little old Mexico again. We're meeting Silvers at the airport."

"What do you plan to do with us?" Paul asked, knowing the answer even before it was given.

"Take you to Mexico, buddy. Santez has ways of getting rid of people who get in the way." He laughed. "You're bodies won't ever be found!"

Myer finally motioned with the gun. "Come on, lovers—we have a nice long ride ahead of us...and I'm going to enjoy every minute of it. The idea of what I'll have the pleasure of doing to the two of you will make every minute enjoyable. I'll think of something especially good—for both of you!"

He laughed again and jerked the gun toward the door. "Come, dead people!"

MISTRESS OF THE DAMNED; &, DEATH IN HER ARMS

CHAPTER SEVEN

The drive to the airport was a study in deep, depressive silence. Paul was sweating behind the wheel, trying desperately to think of some escape. The man with the gun always had the advantage.

Myer was in the back with Lynn, a smug smile on his face, and with the sure knowledge that it was quite impossible for Paul to do anything to save himself or this woman.

They arrived at the airport to find that Silvers wasn't there, yet, but Myer directed Paul to get his plane out of the hangar. By the time he was finished, Silvers arrived with a couple of other men.

Myer filled Silvers in on the details of what had happened, as Paul finished putting gas in the plane. Silvers approached Paul.

"You made a bad mistake, young man," the man announced in a dangerous friendly voice. "I'm sorry for you!"

Paul stared back, stunned by the man's almost pleasant attitude.

"All I'm doing is helping some poor slobs organize a revolt against a government which is making slaves of their people. What's wrong with that? Their present form of government can't be overthrown every four years, like in America. We have a legal revolt here and can kick out the present government if it hasn't pleased us. This little country I'm helping doesn't have this chance. What's wrong with what I'm doing?"

Paul didn't answer the question, and Silvers moved away, lighting a cigar, then puffing smoke into the thick fog around the airfield.

Myer stepped into the plane and went to the cockpit.

Paul didn't even attempt to warn him not to touch his plane. All of a sudden the plane wasn't important. He didn't even worry about the fog. That was Myer's problem, not his.

Paul and Lynn were hustled into the passenger compartment. They sat close to one another, silent, holding hands.

The takeoff was surprisingly smooth, and once they were a hundred feet up, the fog lifted away.

The long flight seemed like an eternity to Paul. His life blasted before his eyes over and over again. Now, faced with death, everything took on a different meaning. A different glow. Morality, social standards, ethics, all became meaningless.

Finally, the flight came to an end and Myer brought the plane to a stop on the sandy stretch of beach outside the Santez bungalow—the same one where Gina and Paul had conducted their evening orgy.

They were met by a small band of men, armed to the teeth. Paul and Lynn were shoved together and taken to a small room in the guest building. Then the door was bolted from the outside and a guard posted in front.

It was the first time that either of them had had a chance to talk since the sudden appearance of Jack Myer at Lynn's apartment. Lynn collapsed into his arms, trembling. They kissed for a long time, not saying anything until they had broken away.

Lynn cried: 'I'm sorry about this, Paul."

Paul shrugged. "It happened. There's nothing we can do about it. Maybe we'll get a chance to escape. My plane's out there on the beach. If we get a chance, we can find the nearest airport, notify your Federal contact and he'll take it from there!"

Lynn suddenly brightened, "You think that'd be possible? Really possible?"

Paul didn't, but wanted to keep that thought from showing on his face as he said: "Who knows? In any case, we can try."

He stepped to the window. The guard was visible, standing in front of the door. "It's hopeless right now."

Paul turned, shrugged. "We'll have to await developments."

"I think I love you, Paul."

"Only think?" he chuckled, letting his eyes communicate his own very real feelings for her.

"Oh, I know I do," she stated matter of fact. "I'd give anything in the world to change things..."

The sob in her voice brought him to her, frantic to sooth away the pain. For a long time they merely held each other, locking tight together, trapped in their own tormented hell.

Paul was about to tell her how much he loved her, how much she meant to him, when a familiar voice sounded from outside. Paul froze as if slapped in the face. His body went hot and then cold.

What was Gina doing out there? His mind screamed. Softly slipping to the window, Paul tried to listen to the voice.

"You like Gina?" came the soft caressing voice of the Latin whore. There was a silence and then she added: "Come with me..."

There was hot promise in her words.

"I can't!" rasped the guard.

Paul saw what was taking place but couldn't believe his eyes. There was a sudden glint of steel flashing in the moonlight, held in Gina's small right hand.

Hope fired. It didn't seem possible, but now they maybe had a chance. Paul gasped, his lungs expanded, shocked and surprised at what he was witnessing.

The gun in Gina's hand smashed into the man's head. He fell forward without a sound.

The woman moved fast, unlatching the door and hurriedly swinging it open. Her eyes searched the room and spotted Lynn where she was lying on the bed and then found Paul where he stood by the window.

Automatically Paul braced himself for the explosion, for surely it would come. Here was the perfect setup for out and out murder. Gina, a woman who had risked everything to save a man she liked—or maybe even more than liked—now found that he was with another woman. And Gina had a gun in her hand.

For a moment, emotion exploded in Gina's eyes, then she relaxed, a strange resigned expression clouding over her face.

"Hurry. Come!" she said. The words were soft, whispering, and tense. Without a word the two of them followed her.

"Hurry!" Gina ordered sharply, looking in the direction of the bungalow. "We don't have time!"

Paul was still dazed. It seemed incredible that Gina would risk so much to save them. He wondered what could have actually motivated her and why?

They were just at the end of the clearing, about to disappear beyond the view of the house, when Jack Myer loomed suddenly from the pathway like a gigantic shadowy statue of death. He must have been out on the beach, tending the plane. He wasn't at first aware of them.

Paul leaped forward. In one quick movement he disarmed Gina and pressed toward the man.

Myer moved fast, cat-like. He was startled, surprised, but fully dangerous, and able to kill.

Paul felt the impact of a fist hit his face. It was a brutal, painful blow, stunning him. Blackness threatened to take over.

The gun had already fallen from his numbed fingers, and all Paul could think of was that Lynn was doomed if she didn't get away fast.

"Run!" he yelled at the girls.

Out of the corner of his eyes he saw them rushing past. Then he staggered to his feet and swung out at Myer. His blow missed. He felt steel-like hardness hit deep into his gut. Pain flashed stars before his eyes. He doubled over, struggling with the agony and sickness that erupted inside him.

Myer was already shouting toward the house when Paul gained control of himself and fought back the pain and stars clouding vision. His one thought was Lynn.

Charging like a mad bull, Paul rushed the larger man. This time his mind clearly centered on the point of the other's jaw. With all the strength in his arms and body, Paul swung, both hands clasp together He knew that if he didn't connect with a staggering blow, all would be lost.

He had to get past Myer and to the plane. It was their only chance—and they wouldn't get a second one.

Myer sidestepped neatly.

Paul's fist hit empty air and then he felt the impact of hard bone and flesh jar at the point of his jaw. It was like being hit by a charging train. He staggered, blackness blinding his vision. Frantically, he struggled for control. Then another fist slammed into his face, knocking him to the ground.

Somehow Paul managed to see through the haze of pain. He found himself lying face down on the hard cold ground. Desperation gave him the needed strength. His eyes searched the ground and came to rest on the gun that he'd taken from Gina.

Then he saw Jack Myer rushing toward the bungalow, shouting.

The front door opened and Silvers and Santez rushed out, looking at the other man in amazement, as if he were suddenly insane.

Paul reached for the gun, and his fingers curled around it. There wasn't time for anything other than two quick shots in the direction of the three men.

Then he staggered to his feet, rushing toward the beach, down the jungle-surrounded pathway that had been cleared to the house.

Yells followed Paul and then the crack of a gun sounded from behind.

Paul rushed along the path and suddenly broke out onto the sandy beach.

Lynn and Gina were starting to get into the plane as he moved hurriedly toward them. He was within a few feet of the plane when the sound of a gun firing shattered the tropic night again. Two bullets smashed into the side of the plane. He turned, firing at the one rushing him, shouting to the girls to hurry.

His aim had been wild, but it brought the others to a momentary stop.

Paul turned in time to see Gina suddenly double over in agony as a bullet from Myer's gun struck her. She started to slide down toward the sand as he reached out and grabbed her body. Quickly leaping into the plane, he managed to draw Gina in with him. Then closing and bolting the door, Paul gave Lynn the gun, telling her to use it. Then he rushed into the cockpit.

The next moments seemed like an eternity. Paul struggled with the controls trying to force the plane into action before it was sufficiently warmed up.

Slowly the craft started edging forward.

Paul realized that the next moments would be the most dangerous. It was necessary to turn the plane, since there wasn't enough beach in front of him for a take-off. Then the hesitation, while the motors warmed up. In those moments, a well-aimed bullet might bring a sudden end to his escape efforts.

Bullets were already smashing through the cockpit window, inches from Paul's head as he slowly turned the Mary-Lou, heading north, right toward Silvers and his men As he faced north, he saw Myer, Silvers and Santez standing in the middle of the beach, right in line of the take off.

The two engines were coughing terribly in the coldness of the morning, holding back their efforts to heat into full action.

Myer was carefully taking aim.

Paul ducked, flattened below the controls in an attempt to save himself. The impact of glass shattered through the cockpit and a bullet smashed into the wall where his head had been. Paul looked through the window as two more bullets missed his head by inches. A score of men were coming from the jungle now. Several carried sub-machine guns. That was all he needed.

Paul's eyes flicked to the propellers. They sputtered slightly and then caught fire.

In that instant Paul made a desperate decision.

He gunned the plane and it started quickly forward. At first it seemed to creep and then slowly began to gain speed. Bullets were smashing into the cockpit all around him. Then pain seared Paul's right arm. Shock numbed him. Fighting the pain, Paul pressed the Mary-Lou forward. It was his last possible chance.

The plane finally raced toward the three men standing on the beach. They were scattering to get out of the way of the charging aircraft as it rushed right at them.

A wonderful feeling of satisfaction shuddered through Paul as he watched several men smashed to their deaths against the wings of his plane. Then as the sound of machine guns shattered the air, the plane slowly started to lift, struggling its way into the sky.

Paul then saw the rocks again, threateningly high. The plane wasn't rising fast enough. Bullets tore into the left wing, tracing an uneven line across its width. Then all at once the rocks were before him and Paul strained back on the wheel and the plane slowly nosed upwards, just tipping the jagged death which had threatened to destroy their escape and their lives in those last moments.

Paul kept rising until they were over a thousand feet into the air. Then he set the plane to automatic pilot, stepping back into the passenger compartment.

Lynn came into his arms, crying. It was a long time before either of them spoke.

Finally they broke away from each other.

Paul searched for Gina, who he was sure must be dead or dying.

He spotted her. She was sitting in one of the seats, a red smear at her left side, but she smiled across at him.

"I fixed things real good," she observed, happily. "Where to, now?"

Paul laughed. "To the United States authorities. They'll see that this thing is cleared up! It's their business now," Paul announced, feeling suddenly happy with relief.

"And," Gina inquired, "What about me?"

"You'll be all right. We'll see to that. Tell them what you did and—they can do a lot of things with that information ... you'll find a place for yourself—but not the kind of life you have already lived!"

Lynn gripped his arm and he turned, looking at her.

"Well," he said, "when we get back—I think a little trip is in order for the two of us." He pulled Lynn into the cockpit and closed the door after her. Lynn's eyes questioned him, startled, and surprised by his sudden action.

"Well, you don't want to live in sin all your life, do

you?" Paul laughed, taking Lynn into his arms. "I think Lynn Phillips will suit you pretty damned well!"

He didn't say anything after that for a long, long time. Their lips were fused together, communicating in the most intimate way possible her binding acceptance of his words.

When they parted from the embrace, the morning sun was slowly beginning to creep over the eastern horizon.

"See?" Paul told her, "you never know what a new day might bring. Last night we were ready to accept death—and today—well, we have a new...a lifetime together."

Lynn teased him with her eyes. "What makes you think I want a man like you?"

He laughed at that. "You don't have any choice, Lynn. My Lynn."

She merely murmured happily, and let him pull her into his arms one more time.

"I do love you," Lynn said as they slipped into the control chairs.

Paul settled down behind the pilot's seat and corrected the course toward Los Angeles and Lynn and was happy for the first time in her life.

Los Angeles, Lynn thought, *was where their world would really begin.*

And, of course, Paul was thinking exactly the same thing.

BOOK TWO

Death in Her Arms

Prologue

The room didn't look like a jail cell, because it wasn't made to be. Yet, for the purposes of keeping the man under arrest, it might have been just that. There was a police guard standing outside, and any attempt to escape would have been useless.

The man's name was Hank Turner. Handsome, tall and well built. He paced the floor like a mountain cat who had felt the freedom of living in paradise and now, for the first time, was caged, held ready to be shipped to some unknown zoo.

He ran a large hand through the crop of curly red hair that hadn't been combed for hours. Several ugly bruises marked his face, but he hardly noticed them any more.

His mind was seething, tormented almost beyond sanity.

Everything will be all right, he kept telling himself over and over. This was merely a routine investigation, and the killing *had* been accidental.

But even then, Mr. Hank Turner—Where was it going to get you? He thought in anguish.

It was merely a routine arrest, until the police could establish one way or another, where the guilt lay for the death of García Flynn. The fact that Hank had killed the man was self-evident. Nobody denied that. The fact that it had been justified was something completely different. The only witnesses were two beautiful women. One was dead; the other couldn't be found. And until they found her, they only had his word about what happened.

Hank pulled out another cigarette and lit it nervously.

Two women, complete opposites. One was a beautiful Latin girl who had never gotten much out of life but a raw deal, but whose free and wild desire for men had pulled him innocently into a life and death conflict.

It all seemed childish and incredible, now that he looked back on those few days. Everything had been purely innocent on his part. He was out for a good time, a moment to escape and find himself. To reason out his life and its direction, which had seemed aimless and unfulfilling.

Really quite ironic.

This was all too perfect. He had a successful career as a bum and con man desperately attempting to find "happiness" and finally having it handed to him. But only to be loused up by other events, which had nothing to do with him except for the fact that on one of his drunken binges, he'd taken a strange girl to his rooms and made love to her. A pick-up tramp. That had been the beginning of it all. A dumb act considering today's dangers and need for safe sex. He could only blame the liquor and his deeply depressed mood. Plus the loneliness that needed filling.

And the other woman—the woman who mattered and who had shown him the magic of real love—what about her? She had come too late. If only he hadn't wakened to discover Vicky López in bed with him. If only he had stayed in the cabin that night. That was the turning point, the moment when it had all started. Waking and finding Vicky López in the bed, lying next to him.

Sitting down on the narrow bed, he lighted another cigarette and thought back....

Chapter One

It had started some days before, waking with the dry taste of a desert in his mouth.

Hank Turner twisted nervously in bed; a feeling of restlessness engulfed him. At first he couldn't remember exactly what had happened the night before. It was all in a blurry alcoholic haze, still unclear. Then he spotted the curving form on the bed next to him.

A dark frown twisted his lips as he raised a hand to brush back a lock of red hair from his wide, darkly tanned forehead. Then, quickly sitting up, he studied the fine, sensual features of the olive skinned woman sleeping quietly next to him. He couldn't get his eyes off her stunning face.

She was quite attractive, he thought, *dark, tall, sensual.* Long flowing locks of blue-black hair disappeared under the sheets, inviting his desire to see the rest of her.

Grunting softly to himself, Hank smiled and then slipped out of bed, moving toward the bathroom. He was on automatic, reacting without consideration for anything other than the moment.

His mouth felt thick and gummy and there was a light hammering at the back of his head. But that wasn't unusual. During the last couple of weeks he'd managed to make the bar scene a habit in the wee hours of the night. Usually with some broad, like the one lying on his bed.

But last night he'd apparently picked himself up a beaut, he laughed silently, still confused as to what had happened.

The woman looked Mexican, and was darkly attractive enough to get her share of men. He couldn't wonder about what had happened last night. Memory was vague.

He'd have to find out what it had been like with her. But not until he had erased the fuzzy numbness from his brain and body.

Washing his face with ice cold water from the tap, he studied himself in the small mirror. The man staring back had chiseled features; the large face was strongly muscled and had a hard used look about it. Red hair seemed to give it strength and a solid appearance.

That image was a false front, hiding the real torment seething under it.

Sighing, Hank couldn't decide whether he needed a shower, a drink, or some coffee.

He glanced at his watch. It was only 9:30 in the morning.

A little early for whiskey, he reflected, vaguely irritated by the thought. Hank paused, then leaned his head out the door to look at the woman lying on the bed. For a moment he stared, then decided it wasn't too early for a drink, after all.

Drying his face, he stepped back into the bedroom and crossed to the small kitchenette kindly equipped in each of the small cabins by Bennings' Lodge management. Reaching for the half empty bottle on the sink, he raised it to his lips and gulped. For a moment he stood there, letting the whiskey settle in his stomach. Then he took a deep breath, moved back into the motel room, stepped to the side of the large double bed and looked down at the beautiful form sleeping there.

A sleeping woman could always be such a lovely image to watch. And she was quite a looker.

It was pleasant to watch the falling and rising of her generous chest, observing the quiet movement of her breathing which he could easily follow even through the bed covers.

A quiet moan broke from her lips and then she suddenly opened her eyes.

It seemed to take her a moment to focus on him, then she smiled. Full lips parting to reveal white even teeth.

After a moment of considering him, she stretched slightly, a natural act that was so sensual to watch that he

90

couldn't keep his eyes off her. Even under the sheets the woman's body showed a lush fullness that caused an instant response to race through his own.

Then she sat up, the sheet sliding down to reveal full, well shaped breasts that proudly stood firmly in place.

She whispered in a rich low voice, "Hello there, lover boy."

"Hello," he greeted, slowly sitting down on the bed. "Beautiful woman."

She arched an eyebrow and then smiled once more. There was all the warmth of a tropical tornado in her gaze as it fairly feasted on him. "That's not what you called me last night."

"What'd I call you last night?"

"A wild tigress!" The woman laughed throatily and then slid her arms around his neck. "Don't you remember, lover?"

"Nothing!" Hank let his hands touch her shoulders, the flesh was soft, warm.

"Nice," she offered, throatily, lips half parted.

His fingers glided around the woman's back and firmly drew her up toward him. "Wish I did, too."

"You were pretty drunk."

She moved against him, hugging close.

For a long while they didn't say anything, just aware of this intimate first contact. Somehow it was quite nice, holding her that way, almost like a dear friend he had known for a long time. Not a total stranger.

Hank felt little tremors move through her body, and suddenly she tightened against him.

"You were really good last night," she murmured. "I bet you're even better sober."

Her lips moved to his, lightly at first. After that she became what he had called her the night before; all clawing wild beast devouring her mate in a savage dance of unrestrained passion.

* * * * * * *

Later they rested in each other's arms. Then, slowly,

Hank moved from her.

She was the kind of woman a man needed at one time or another in his life—the kind that was purely sensual, a savage animal. Mere escape.

He had been escaping from himself and his past and his family all his life, so he knew the meaning of escape. As a teenager he had been given too much, until the recession had hit Wall Street and his family lost their major investments. Then he'd had the hard life. His father had taken to drinking, and finally it killed him. His mother eventually sought quick love affairs with well vested men for escape and recapturing a sense of the good life. Then things went downhill and a couple of years ago she had settled in with a rather low class, mean man with little style, who had a taxi cab. That had ended when the man was killed in an auto accident. Since then dear mother had disappeared east with the insurance money.

Life had been a bunch of crap during those years. He'd escaped from it all as best he could. There were the women, of course. Only drugs had been a no-no. And until the emotional depression started waving into his life, he'd managed to keep the drinking within a reasonable control. His body had seemed like a temple to keep in as good as shape as possible. Women like men with hard muscles and lean body.

Yes, Hank thought, *you're an expert on escaping.*

He wondered who was keeping his dear sweet mother now. He hadn't heard from her for several years, and didn't care if he ever saw her again. At fifteen he'd run away from the cheap tenement house where he had been living with her since his father had managed to kill himself with cheap wine. There had been the series of odd jobs until he joined the Army. He'd been given training in Special Services, but during his service in Germany he never did much of anything but fool around. If it had lasted longer things might have been different. But a nasty drinking scene had ended in a bar fight and then there was some confusion that involved a woman he didn't even remember and an auto accident that damaged his right leg pretty badly at the time. Apparently he had come to the defense of the woman who was being bullied by the man next to her. Turned out the lady in the question was the daughter of some embassy mucky muck. In the hospital he was visited by a strange man who had slipped him a roll of bills, saying: "She felt bad about all this! Her way of thanking you." He never really knew why or how, but he was given a quick medical discharge to get him carted off back to the states. That ended any Special Service action. But it sure as hell taught him how to defend himself—and how to kill—even with his bare hands. The money the woman had given him was enough to bankroll some investments that turned out lucky. For all practical purposes he was a non-person to the military—a permanent member of the civilian population. Things were never quite the same after that. Life had drifted into a loose hazy blur over the last few years.

But he found no escape or answers to what he was or where he was going.

From then on he'd managed to see a good part of the country, ending up in Los Angeles with still enough money to invest in a couple of small Hollywood deals that paid off. And finally, to get married to a young starlet who had more curves than brains and temper than talent. That had been a mistake. They divorced when he learned she was playing the casting couch game with would-be producers and power brokers. Cheap promises for a swift screwing on the couch. After that, he'd figured, the best way to get money back on investments was to do quick films. He'd done some fast sex flicks, nearly X-rated, then invested in a friend's production company, which turned out to be putting out XXX films. He pulled out of that fast. It all lasted long enough to get him too close to some seedy productions. But it had given him enough money to run once more. He'd already formed a production company which produced nothing; a shell for future business, which he wasn't sure he wanted to do anything with. So he'd backed off, taken some trips, and drank a bit too much. And run.

Run to nowhere.

Running into the arms of a hot chick like he'd just been enjoying.

Sighing, Hank turned and looked at the woman next

to him. She was sitting up in bed, smoking, staring at the far wall. So she was a smoker, too.

"Did I get your name last night?" he inquired as he sat up and reached for a pack of cigarettes on the bed between them. Lighting one, he took a deep drag and let out a thin stream of smoke.

She smiled and turned in his direction. "Now that's really something! We didn't even exchange names."

"I'm Hank Turner."

"Victoria López. But call me Vicky. Everybody does …even enemies. I figure after all…this…between us…we have the right to call ourselves friends."

"Why not?" He reached out and gently patted her hand. "Here on vacation?"

"For a few weeks." She looked away, as if avoiding eye-contact.

"Alone, I take it?"

"Not really…" came her uneasy reply. "Well…with you right now."

He felt a stab of warning eat at his guts, mixed with regret. "Not alone, then?"

"Alone for now, but García Flynn will be coming up in a couple of days—"

"A friend?"

"Well…let's say we're past the holding hands bit."

"What a shame."

Her eyes flashed for a moment with violently raw anger, then she said, "No man has his tag on me!"

"But you don't think he should know about this?" he inquired, shrugging. "I take it."

"He's a jealous and dangerous man."

"Why take chances, then?" Hank asked.

"I can't stand still for long. I have to have…something to keep me busy. You know…something nice like…like you. For instance!"

She smiled brightly, then her lips parted in a more sensual way and they moved slowly towards him.

Grinning, he reached out, pulled Vicky to him for a prolonged, almost tender kiss.

Her hands clutched at his shoulders, then slid down

94

along his hard muscular arms. She smiled warmly, letting her arms stroke his muscles, run over his chest. "You're very strong…I like that."

He grinned. Let his eyes take in her full breasts where they just touched him. "I like that…"

They both laughed—delighted at the mutually complimentary verbal exchange.

She said: "I almost believe you!"

"So do I!" he teased.

"Me or you?" she giggled.

"Hey…playing with words?" he challenged, pleased.

"I play with all kinds of things! Can you imagine that?" She laughed at that, then slipped out of his arms. "Looks like we're pretty nicely matched!"

"How's that?"

"We enjoy…playing!" she murmured, pulling his hands around to the back of her neck. Then their lips met again—this time with greater urgency and need.

It was early evening before Vicky left Hank Turner's cabin to go to the rooms she had rented in the Hotel Lodge.

The afternoon had been a series of heated embraces, interrupted only for cigarette breaks or gulps from the bottle of whiskey which he had brought into the bedroom.

After a long shower, Hank dressed in slacks and a white shirt. Pulling on a warm jacket, he stepped from his cabin and breathed deeply of the clear, cool mountain air.

This is the life, he thought contentedly as the clean air filled his lungs, refreshing his body and giving him a sudden sense of momentary well-being. Vicky López had been really fun and damned good for him. Yet there was the inner sense of not being completely satisfied, as if he had missed something which she couldn't give. There had been all that passion, and even a tender hot joy in one another; but no real loving tenderness or deeply meaningful affection.

Even if she was simply great fun, it was obviously limited to that, and she had her jealous lover coming around soon to keep her at arms distance.

He really didn't need getting involved with her.

Yet the woman was a real keeper insofar as how they related, how they had socially and physically intercoursed the afternoon away. They were like two delighted wild animals in mutual heat.

But it was all empty; just like his life had been.

A woman like Vicky could kill a few delicious hours—but it all ended up the same afterwards.

Hank realized that his need was for emotional fulfillment—a loving relationship. It always came down to that.

The emptiness. Isolation.

His eyes took in the scenery as he started for the dining hall in the Lodge. He noted green pines, the bold, naked rocks, the little stream to the right of the path. Low white clouds accented the dark blue of the evening sky. It was getting close to the snow season.

Stepping up to the stone entranceway to the *Bennings Lodge,* he pushed through the door, hardly noticing the warmth of the fireplace across the room. His eyes quickly searched through the lobby.

Bertha Jones was standing behind the hotel desk. She was somewhere in the middle or late thirties; still not too bad looking, if a man went in for the plump full body. She was the type of lonely female who hungered for male companionship.

Her hands quickly motioned to Hank.

He stepped to the desk. "How're things?"

Bertha smiled and leaned forward.

"You certainly put one on, last night." Her bantering tone was mingled with a hint of longing. "Quite a...night with that woman? I bet! Lucky her! I'd have traded places in a flash!"

"Golly, Bertha, I'd have...well, enjoyed a berth with you if you'd just asked."

"Sure. I'm just your type. I noticed." She puffed up her breasts in a playful self-mockery. "That lady had some! And you couldn't get her eyes off her long enough to notice hot sexy me."

She laughed at that, trying to make a joke of her words.

"Maybe we should do something about that someday."

"Sure. Of course. Bet it'll never happen."

96

"Never bet your life on that!"

"Thanks. But…admit it. I'm simply not your type. And that woman you were with last night was. In spades!"

"Did I make a blasted fool of myself?"

Her eyes flashed a little more seriously. "Well, I just have a feeling about her, I'd be careful, Hank. There are other women around."

He studied her for a long moment. The direction of the conversation had drifted, changed from light banter to something far more serious. Maybe even dangerous.

She shot him a smile. "Honey, I'm just a foolish tavern dame looking out for her happy customers. There are a lot of women around without any…bad vibes…if you know what I mean. Miss López isn't a loner. I'm just saying…consider your options."

"Who would you suggest?"

A sudden flush appeared on her chubby cheeks as she nervously brushed aside a lock of white-blonde hair. "Look, Hon, I wouldn't tell you what to do—that's your business."

"Any new action?"

She frowned. "There's a Miss Lee, who checked in today, but nothing new that might interest you. If that's what you mean." Her tone was a little biting. "I don't know why I let you con me into giving information on the competition, honey."

"There's no competition where you're concerned," he laughed, patting Bertha on the cheek. "Well, see you around, Bertie."

Hank moved into the dimly lit cocktail lounge, letting his eyes get used to the darkness as they drifted around the room. There weren't many people there this early. Then he spotted a young, attractive woman sitting at the bar. He hadn't seen her before. He was immediately drawn to her—something about her was like a powerful magnet.

His gaze took in her trim figure, the almost boyish shape of her body. The short Italian haircut was swept neatly back. Her profile was delicate, but with pouting lips, quiet intriguing. He wondered if she might be the Miss Lee that Bertha had mentioned.

Hank crossed to the barstool next to her, sat down

and ordered a martini. Then he "accidentally" brushed the woman's arm.

"Sorry. I didn't—" He suddenly broke off. Something in that brief physical contact had jarred him, something he could neither see nor touch. It was a mixture of emotion and strange calm, of excitement and numbness. Never before had the sight or touch of a woman given him such a jolt or cast such a quick spell.

His breath caught up inside him, hanging in his throat like a large hard ball. His nerves came alive with a tingling sensation. These were feelings he had read about, heard about, but never quite believed were real. Feelings which he attempted to brush aside as imagination. But he couldn't.

It wasn't that she was more beautiful than any other woman in the world, for he had seen many, slept with too many. But there was a certain "atmosphere" about her, which left him oddly breathless.

She was strikingly attractive in a feminine yet boyish way. That was the most he could say for her.

She stared back at him, a little shyly at first, then a slow, slightly crooked smile spread across her soft velvet lips.

"That's all right. I guess you didn't mean it." Her voice was low and rich, vibrant, almost trembling.

She feels it too, he told himself, still amazed at what was happening.

She kept her eyes on him for a long moment, and then finally lowered them to her cocktail glass.

Hank allowed a short silence to follow, then asked:

"You arrived today?"

It was a moment before she answered. "Yes, but how'd you know?"

"Been here for some weeks. I'd have noticed you before."

"That's quite a line."

"Staying long?"

There was a pause. She bit her lower lip nervously, then her doe-like brown eyes moved to his and locked there. "For a couple of weeks. On vacation—"

"Alone?"

98

"Why?" Her question was startled, edgy.

"Just…well…wondering. Interested?"

She nodded, but didn't say anything. Instead, she took a sip of her drink.

"By the way, I'm Hank." Silence answered him. "You're Miss Lee?"

"How did you know?" she demanded, amazed.

"Have my ways."

She stared at him for a long moment and then said, "I don't know what you're after, Mister—" Her tone had turned to ice.

"Hank Turner."

"Mister Turner, you're wasting your time."

She hurriedly finished her drink, paid the bartender, got up and walked out of the lounge without another word.

The bartender grinned at Hank. "Looks like you just got a chunk of ice mixed with your warm line."

"Damned pretty chunk," Hank observed, grinning. "Guess it might take time to thaw out."

"That kind of girl might not thaw."

"Give me time. They all fall, at one time or another." But Hank was shaken by her sudden cold front.

"Think she's a little skinny for your tastes. You seem to go for the more shapely types, I've noticed!"

He resented that, and only with effort remained pleasant, saying: "I'd like that kind of change."

The bartender grinned, then walked away.

Hank sat there for a long time, his thoughts stormy over the woman. He'd never had anything shake him so much. It scared him.

Yet he was going to cut through that coldness. He'd been sure she had felt the electric spark between them. It was like two elements of a bomb making contact and exploding into life. He'd felt the bolt—fully.

That evening he tried to find her, but she wasn't anywhere around. He remembered Vicky and considered finding out wherever she was hiding; then shook his head. He wasn't in the mood. Finally he returned to his cabin with a bottle of whiskey and got quietly drunk, alone.

Chapter Two

Hank was outside and strangely sober the next morning; he was starting for the lodge for breakfast when Bertha Jones swung up beside him. She was dressed in warm jeans, a leather jacket and thick wool gloves.

"Hi, love? Who wasted you last night?"

"I look that bad?"

"No. Really rather nice in a dragged out way! Hung over?"

"Maybe."

"Some lady get lucky?" She rubbed her hands together to warm them.

"Lucky?" he asked, all innocence.

"Well, you know." She touched his arm. "Oh, my … I better not do *that*!"

"What?"

"You're really hard…makes a girl wonder…"

"Wonder about what, young lady of the innocent smile?"

"Don't push me…I melt easily!"

"Not touching you!" He swung his hands up in the air, helplessly. "I'm innocent."

"My damn luck!"

He winked, playfully, almost evilly, letting his eyes seem to feast on her chubby body as if lingeringly hungry.

"Oh, *stop* that. You naughty man!" she complained, blushing suddenly.

"Well, if you insist!" He hugged the woman, gently. "You're a nice lady!"

"Hey, there's nice and there's nice. And I know the difference." As he released her. she added: "And I bet you

101

were dancin' with the difference last night. Lucky lady, huh?"

"Not really. Just alone with my bottle and myself."

She laughed at that, shrugged, then added: "Well, it's nice to know that even the Champ has an evening alone."

They were quiet for a moment as she glanced at the sky.

He followed her gaze.

The early morning air was like a chilly hand pressing around the shadowy pines surrounding the lodge. The sky was darkening with heavy clouds.

"Well, Bertie, it looks like snow season."

Her eyes twinkled. "It can also be the sign of rain, or wind. It's storm weather, too. You never can tell."

Just then the woman who had iced Hank's advances the day before, stepped up to them.

"Hello, Miss Lee," Bertha greeted.

"Bobbie," the woman corrected, smiling. But she seemed to politely ignore Hank.

Bertha asked her: "Coming on the company hike?"

"What's that?"

"Oh, just a tour of the grounds, around here. Some of the guests like to explore a bit."

"Where to?" Bobbie inquired.

"There are some caves a couple of miles in," Bertha quickly informed her. "The scenery's beautiful,"

"I don't know. I'm not much at hiking. How long will it take, and when do you leave?"

"We'll be gone all morning. Leave in about an hour."

"Then I'll have time to eat first?"

"Why, of course, honey," Bertha said. "We meet right here, in front of the lodge."

Bobbie Lee nodded and moved toward the wood framed building.

"She's an odd one," Bertha observed, thoughtfully looking up at Hank. She noted how he was watching the woman disappear into the lodge. "Oh. So you're interested?"

"Well..." he smiled, but didn't look away from the door where Bobbie had disappeared. "You won't play, so what can I do?"

102

Bertha considered that, then suddenly poked him in the ribs. "Are there any limits to your wanton madness?"

"Tell me about her," Hank suggested, seriously. "Know anything at all?"

"You *are* interested. WOW! YIKES! And all that stuff!"

"You're chatting on the net too much!" he laughed. "Yikes and Wow! Tell me. Anything at all?"

"Well, she is a writer, and you know how they are. Asked to be left alone. Said she wasn't particularly interested in group activities. But…maybe she's joining us after all."

"Interesting," he considered, thoughtfully.

Bertha shrugged. "Well, I gotta get along. Things to organize for the hike. See you later? Coming with us?"

"Maybe. Depends."

Bertha walked off and Hank went into the coffee shop. Quickly searching the room, he spotted Bobbie Lee sitting alone at the far end of the counter. He moved to the chair next to hers.

"Hello," he greeted warmly. "Can I call you Bobbie, too?"

Bobbie turned her slender face in his direction and gazed into Hank's eyes. "You certainly don't play around, do you?"

"Well, I wouldn't put it just that way," he countered, trying to be light.

"Neither would I." She simply glanced at her hands, then at him. "You're not a very subtle man, are you?"

"Subtle?"

She looked uncertain as their eyes met, lingeringly. "Oh, nothing!"

"There's *nothing* wrong with being friendly, is there?"

"That depends on what you call friendly," she pointed out icily.

"Friendly is friendly."

"That depends on what sex you are."

"Sister, you have one hell of a chip on your shoulder," he snapped back, a bit harsher than he meant it to sound.

103

"Men are men. Women are women. Men want one thing. Women want another."

"Now that's deep!" he chuckled, trying to be humorous about it. "Bertha said you were a writer. But, that's so deep even I can't understand."

"That's not even funny!" Bobbie said a bit seriously. "And I suppose you didn't mean it…funny."

"Not really." He felt angry with himself. "We're starting out all wrong. Can't we start all over?"

"Where?"

"Well," he shrugged, "men are men and women are women? And there seemed to be some kind of hidden meaning in that description. Wanna explain?"

"Blunt? Frank? Nitty gritty?"

"How nitty or gritty can it be? Sure. Shoot! Just don't aim for the heart! That's taken!"

"All you men want is a quick thrill."

"Well, I'm thrilled!" he laughed, mockingly. "To the heart, to be frank."

"At what?" she actually sounded surprised, puzzled.

"By just being here with you, of course. Natch."

Confused, a flush touching her cheeks, she blurted: "You know what I mean. Men just want … sex!"

It was such a cuttingly hard remark, so serious, that he felt as if she'd slapped him. Maybe because she'd shot her point right into his mind.

Hank blinked, stunned. This was the most intriguing woman he had met for years.

"What, in heaven's name, gave you that idea?"

"Now come on, Mr. Turner. I wasn't born yesterday," Bobbie exclaimed.

"All I'm interested in is being friendly. I'd like to become your friend, but you're fighting all the way." Somehow those words felt lame even to him. But they were the best he could do.

"You're not my friend. A friend is somebody who'll really help you if you need help. You're just a man trying to pick up with a woman. That's all. Nothing more. And I don't see why you waste your time with me. To be honest, I'm not interested."

104

For a moment, red anger flashed through Hank. "Okay, Miss Lee. You've finally made your point. So we'll have to leave it at that!"

He stood and went down to the other end of the counter. When the waitress came, he ordered coffee, ham and eggs, and a breakfast steak.

He was still fuming about Bobbie Lee when Vicky López walked in and glided over to the counter chair next to his. "Well, howdy, stranger. Mind if I keep you company?"

He felt a warm reaction to her presence. "Why not? I sure could use a little warmth."

"What does that mean?"

"A cold day, that's all," Hank announced, keeping his eyes away from Bobbie Lee. "What you been doing?"

"Sleeping it off."

"When does your buddy arrive?"

"Tomorrow."

Hank sipped his coffee, trying to think of something to say. He was startled when Vicky tapped him on the shoulder.

She pointed to Bobbie Lee. "Who's she?"

"Why?" Hank felt nervousness flutter through him.

"She's been staring at me in the strangest way."

"That's Miss Lee."

"Oh, you know her?"

"Not really."

Vicky was silent for a moment, and then said: "I'm glad."

Hank's food came then and he started to eat, trying hard to keep his mind off Bobbie Lee.

He carried on a light conversation with Vicky; and at first nothing more was said about García Flynn.

After they had finished eating and were sipping coffee, Vicky pointedly remarked, "Why don't we make the most of the day?"

"How's that?" he laughed, playing the innocent.

"Don't game-play me, lover boy," Vicky snapped.

"Okay, what do you have in mind? I was planning on the little hike, myself."

"Okay!" Vicky exclaimed. "Then when we return we

can have a..."

She took hold of his arm, fingers squeezing very firmly into the muscle there.

"I wanna have more of you," she whispered almost musically into his ear. "That was fun...us, together!"

The woman's eyes were openly bright, truly admiring as they glazed into his. "What do ya say?"

"I say.... Hey, hey!" he laughed.

She giggled in delight. "Make hay while the sun rises. All night long, singing our song of wanton lust together."

"You're actually musical!" he noted, deciding this was just want he needed to take the bitter hurt Bobbie Lee had crushed down on him.

Screw Bobbie Lee, he thought, annoyed by the realization that's exactly what he would love to do in the flesh.

Vicky's hand on his arm, actually stroking it, brought his mind back to the woman. "You're just what I needed!"

"Now that's just what a woman loves to hear! You really make me feel wanted."

"Believe me, you are just want I need!" he announced with decision.

"We are matched to mate," she whispered, playfully. "Glad we have time to do it again...later we can't, you know."

He frowned, wondering just what she meant.

"Once he's around, we act like strangers." She squeezed his arm again. "And that's gonna be as hard as that is...for me, anyway!"

She was both serious and somewhat playful.

As if guessing his uncertainty, she merely said: "Nobody will tell him anything...and what he doesn't know won't hurt. And I'm not the talky kind. I promise you. What happens between us stays between us!"

He nodded, then paid the bill for the two of them, and helped Vicky López from her chair.

* * * * * * *

They had been walking through the mountains which

surrounded Bennings Lodge for well over an hour, moving in the little valleys between rocky hills, pushing past brush and trees, up narrow pathways and over rocks, climbing higher by the minute. The air was becoming increasingly colder, and Hank shivered as the clouds started gathering.

His legs were already feeling the effects of the hike. It had been a long time since he'd walked over such territory.

"What you thinking about?" Vicky asked, suddenly breaking into his thoughts.

"Nothing. Really. What made you ask?"

"Oh, who knows? Maybe just making conversation. You've been so quiet."

"Sorry. If its conversation you want…how about a few Qs & As?" Hank asked, helping Vicky along a narrowed portion of the pathway up the side of the hill.

"Mine or yours?"

Considering that, he suggested, "Why don't you tell me something about yourself?"

"What do you want to know?"

"Whatever. Start at the beginning?" he suggested.

"That's a bit…much. But…a bit later will do. Okay?"

"Shoot away! I'm all ears!"

"I don't think that's quite true, lover!" She pointedly looked down along his body, hesitating meaningfully to make her point. "I think there's more to you than ears."

"What's wrong with them?" he wondered.

"Nothing a girl wouldn't wanna whisper all kinds of intimate…well, anyway…that's all for later!" She teased him with a light touch on the cheek.

"I'd rather you tell me your life story. For now." He took her hand in his, gently squeezing the warm fingers.

"Growing up," Vicky said matter-of-factly, "was … not a party!"

"Rough time?"

"Rough time. You can say that again. I don't want to go through that again. No mother, no dad. They were both gone. Only an aunt and uncle. Fruit pickers. We were fruit pickers. I learned early in life that the only way a woman was going to survive in the world was to climb over other people. Guess I did a little climbing. I got out of that rat hole,

107

but fast!"

"I guess things are hard for everyone," Hank said. "One time or another."

They walked along the ledge for about twenty minutes, and finally Bertha brought their climb to a stop. She pointed up the pathway. "That's where we're headed."

To Hank, with his tired and protesting muscles, it looked like a long way. He wasn't disappointed. It was a difficult climb. The pathway narrowed to a little over a foot for a while, but widened towards the end. After that, the rest was easy. They were able to easily move along the almost level path to the cave opening, which appeared like a black blotch on the face of the mountain.

Bertha stopped before the entrance and motioned the others to step in close.

"We have to light our way. There's a lantern inside. I'll get it and then we can continue." She disappeared and then returned a moment later.

"Come on in," she told them, holding the light so that everybody could see the inside of the entrance's sandstone walls.

As Hank moved into the cave he had the feeling of stepping into a world of hidden shadows, of devils and of death. It was like being placed inside the center of the earth. From the ceiling, icicle-shaped stalactites dripped eerily onto their counterparts reaching up from the floor of the cave.

"Quite a place," he heard Bobbie Lee exclaim.

Vicky hissed softly in his ear, "I don't see that it was worth all the effort."

"Don't be silly," Hank told her. "It was the walk we came out for—not the caves."

Vicky laughed and then pushed accidentally against his back. The soft nearness of her was startling, out of tune with the brooding atmosphere of the cavern.

A low moan sounded from the cave entrance.

"What was that?" Vicky demanded.

"Just the wind," Hank whispered.

Bertha stepped past them, lighting the way. "Come on, you people. There's a lot to see, and it's starting to get windy."

108

"Shouldn't we turn back?" somebody asked.

"It ought to be okay," Bertha told them.

A depression settled over Hank as they moved through the cave. It took them about twenty minutes to see what there was—which wasn't much. Finally they circled back and started for the entrance. As they neared the opening of the cave, the sound of moaning grew louder. Hank saw that the trees on the opposite side of the canyon were bending under the force of the wind.

Silence gathered around the cold entrance.

"What now?" Bobbie Lee asked, frightened. She was standing next to Bertha.

"We go down. We can't stay here."

"Won't it be dangerous in that wind?" Vicky wanted to know.

"Yes, but we have a long rope here in the cave. Everything for an emergency." Bertha laughed, but sounded a little forced. She disappeared into the darkness and returned with a rope. "Well, everybody in line. I'll tie the rope around your waists. I'll lead. And Mr. Brown, who has done a lot of mountain climbing, will tail."

Fifteen minutes later they started in single file along the face of the cliff. Bobbie Lee was in front of Hank and Vicky, behind him. A man was between Bobbie and Bertha.

They were starting across the narrow foot-wide ledge when Bobbie suddenly stumbled and fell forward, dragging Hank with her.

For a horrible moment Hank felt he was going to die.

His head hit the side of the cliff and a sick nausea flushed through him. He twisted in the bottom of that spinning whirlpool for several long moments before his head cleared and his eyes opened. He was hanging half over the ledge. Bobbie Lee, below him, was quietly limp.

"Bobbie!" he managed to call. She didn't answer.

"Bobbie!" he cried.

Then Hank was aware of being dragged upwards. He felt hands helping him to his feet, then Bobbie Lee followed.

"Is she all right?" a man asked.

Bertha was examining Bobbie when the young woman opened her eyes. After a moment she became aware

109

of her surroundings, then she moaned and gently touched her ankle.

"I think it's broken," she explained.

Bertha examined it and shook her head. "Just a slight sprain. It'll be all right after a while. But you can't come down with us. There's a helicopter at the Ranger Station. Somebody should stay up here with you."

It took only a second for Hank to impulsively offer to stay.

This was a perfect chance to get to first base with Bobbie Lee.

Vicky frowned angrily, and Hank forced himself to shrug, as if surprised by his own offer. For a moment he thought she was going to offer to stay with them, but she remained silent.

Bobbie's stony, blank expression gave no hint as to her feelings in the matter.

Ten minutes later Hank and Bobbie were sitting inside the cave, watching the others start out for Bennings Lodge.

Chapter Three

The wind was beginning to tighten into a gale, twisting through the canyon, whipping the distant trees as if slapping them with an invisible hand, bringing a cold chill into the cave entrance. The sky had darkened to a gray ugliness, gathering together its strength like some eerie mistress of destruction. They had been there for some time alone, silent, just sitting a bit distantly.

But with all the depressing elements, which were settling over the world outside the cave, Hank felt unreasonable joy at the situation. He was alone with Bobbie Lee.

He wanted to reach out and touch her, comfort her. But didn't move to her. There was a long silence.

Finally Hank took out a pack of cigarettes. "Want one?"

"Thanks." After a moment she asked, "Why'd you stay?"

It was such a strange question. To him it was obvious. He wanted to be with her; get to know her. He wanted to say that and a lot more. But instead he decided on a lie. "I don't know, really."

Silence settled back over them. He tried to think of some way to resume the conversation, but words just choked up in his throat whenever he looked at Bobbie. Normally his light, joking manner would have satisfied such a situation.

Then, suddenly, as if she felt the need for conversation, Bobbie said, "I've acted pretty badly toward you, haven't I?"

"I suppose so."

"Sorry…I guess."

"Forget it."

"I don't understand you. Not at all."

"I don't understand myself," he told her truthfully, feeling tingling sensations ebb through him. "How could you understand me? Who knows themselves?"

Silence.

The wind howled like a wounded animal that is slowly, painfully dying. Hank could hear the far distant sounds of crackling thunder reach out toward them.

"Looks like a bad storm," Hank observed conversationally.

Bobbie looked suddenly alarmed. She started to say something, then stopped. Her eyes met his and he thought it was possible to read the reflection of his own tangled emotions. But that had to be projection.

"Oh, we'll be all right, don't worry." Hank reached out impulsively, patted her arm.

She tensed at the touch.

He withdrew his hand, even while wanting to hold her, to move her closer. Instead he offered: "We'll be okay."

"Maybe so." Her smile was a forced, muscular movement of her lips. "And I guess...maybe you're all right."

"Just all right?"

"Well..."

"I guess that's some improvement."

She flushed slightly, looked nervously away, said: "I was bitchy, wasn't I?"

"WOW! I'm shocked!" he exploded, laughing.

"Well...okay. I'm sorry. Nice of you to stay here." They eyes met, lingeringly searching.

"Could hardly leave you alone!" he admitted.

"I was a bit surprised, considering that...what's her name?"

"Vicky?"

"Yes. You two were..." She hesitated, bit her lower lip, continued nervously, "well, rather frankly...I figured the two of you were...that she's the kind of woman men.... Well, damn! Is she your lover?"

"WOW again!" he chuckled. "Damned if you aren't a surprise!"

112

Even Bobbie laughed at that, though the embarrassed flush on her face didn't go away. "I'm sorry. None of my business."

"Never mind it all," he offered, wanting to drop Vicky as a topic of conversation between them. He hardly needed to admit what really was or wasn't between them. Not to Bobbie, anyway. Plus, like Vicky had said, what went on between them stayed between them. The less admitted about that situation the better. "Right now...all that counts is...this. You and I. Can't we be friends?"

"Yes. Friends. But that's all." Alarm tinged her voice, but Hank thought he detected an uncertainty in her words. Or was this wishful thinking on his part?

"What are you afraid of?" he impulsively asked.

"What are you talking about?" She was instantly alarmed, a sharp edge hardened her voice.

"Well, to be frank," he told her, deciding once and for all to cut through and come right to the point, "afraid of a man finding you interesting?"

"That's off limits!" she exploded. "And I don't see why it is you men are always after us."

"Well...guess we're just made that way." He tried to make that sound light, bantering.

"Is it all sex?"

"Of course not!" he snapped, actually annoyed. Then tried to recover with: "But that's a good start! A guy has to start somewhere. And...well, to be really frank, you're some hot dish!"

He winked at her, hoping that it would be so blatant that she'd laugh it off.

"What's with you? One moment you're nice—and then you have to ruin everything by getting...oh...getting insulting!" Her face twisted with quick anger. "That really makes me furious! I'm not just some...object to use and dump! Had fun, wham bam—thank you, good bye!"

She stopped abruptly, breathing hard. Then words poured out like bullets, hammering at him in quick succession. "Don't you think of women as people—as thinking and reasoning humans? We're caring, intelligent...damn. I sometimes think the whole human race is so screwed up and...oh, never mind. I mean...I don't like being used and dumped like a...well, want am I saying? What do I mean?"

She paused, added, in more control: "I have other things on my mind than some light social flirtation. Obviously!"

Unreasoning anger flickered through him. It seemed impossible to get on gentle, friendly terms with this exasperating woman. No matter what he tired. And it was quite obvious that some of what she said had nothing to do with him.

"Men aren't the way you think," he finally said, controlling the emotion in his voice. "It's just that it's normal for a guy to show interest in a woman he finds attractive. What's wrong with that?"

She shrugged, started to say something, then closed her lips and looked away.

Defensively he said: "That's the way I am. And if it offends you.... Sorry about that. But that's the way of the world, lady. I look at you and...hell, I have...well if a man wants to kiss a woman, she shouldn't feel insulted about that."

She smiled, suddenly, more warmly. "So..."

"Well, so what?" he exploded, feeling suddenly naked. "So I wanted to kiss you the minute I saw you!"

"Now who's being shocking?" she suddenly laughed. Then just as quickly she grew serious. "That's just want I meant! About you men!"

"And what's wrong with that? It is human nature. Attraction leads to a kiss and from there to..."

"See?" she said, playfully shaking her head. "Right down the road to sex!"

"Well? So what!" he actually snapped, totally crushed and confused. With anybody but her he'd have had a quick retort.

"You call that love?" Bobbie demanded bitingly.

"Geeze, who's talking about...I mean—well, no, of course not."

"Well, there you are. Men want sex. Women want love, I suppose."

"What is love, anyway?" Hank retorted. "Who really knows what it is?"

"It's more than sex."

"Of course. But for a lot of people it is probably just a rationalization of the sex impulse!"

Anger flared in Bobbie's eyes. Her face went livid. "Oh, you're the most impossible human I've ever met! Maybe that's what men think it is. But women think a little differently about it. At least this woman does!"

"Hell, that's what's wrong with the world. You women trying to make impossible rules."

"What's wrong with love?" she fired back. "What's wrong with two people finding something in each other which they need or lack, which makes them a little better—makes their lives a little better?"

"Is that what you call love?" Hank's tone was scornful. "Needing something from another?"

"No. Just part of it. It's affection. It's wanting to help and wanting to take care of somebody. It's the desire to be with someone for the rest of your life. It's not passion. It's the need of two people for each other, to build something lasting and make each partner a little happier. You can't go through life using up everything and then throwing it aside. You have to build something. Create, by building."

"What's wrong with two humans being together for a short time?" he offered, suddenly thoughtful, abruptly thinking about what she had actually said without taking it personally.

Bobbie threw up her hands. "Oh, for God's sake! That's not love—that's lust!"

Hank felt exasperation stab through him. "That is love. Maybe not the kind you demand, expect. But it is a love of sorts. There are all kinds of love. People are born, and as they go through life they need different things at different times. You meet people. Your paths cross, sometimes for a short while, sometimes longer. Who says we have to limit our relations to holding hands? Even at midnight? Or by forcing our paths together, regardless of our ever changing needs?"

"You really believe that is love?" she asked, her eyes searching his.

"It *can* be love. We're here only once, and should

115

make the most of it. Grab hold with our hands and teeth. Struggle with life, fight it, take what we can at the moment and be damned happy when we find some love here or there…and some goodness in life. Things are bad enough to ignore a chanced treasured moment. If I meet a woman I find hot…please forgive me for showing it. I'm single and free. If she feels the same way, why not? And for as long or as short as it might be? Grab it while you can! Before it's too late."

Bobbie sighed, almost sadly. "You're talking about free love."

"No, nothing's free. That's not what I meant," Hank protested "I mean—hell, people should be able to make the most of their lives? Just because some fool society says we shouldn't do this or that…"

"You have to follow the rules," she offered, rather gently.

"Which rules? The Christian world has one set. The Islamic another. And the non-believers even a different system of rules. And some of them clash brutally, dangerously, madness rules there. All this world order and all this hate, hate, hate. If you don't do it my way, then you're the devil."

She laughed at that. "I hardly meant that."

"Well you know what I mean. 9/11 changed things."

"Yes. That's for sure."

"But it underscored something, too. Not everybody can be right, even if they believe they are. What's right at one place is wrong at another. Oh, hell. Forget it!"

"No. Really," she encouraged, "You're starting to sound intelligent!"

"Oh, thanks for small compliments."

"You are very welcomed. Still it doesn't change anything."

He shrugged, hands spreading, as he looked down at them, thinking: "Hell, go back a hundred years and you find it was right to have prostitution. Now it's illegal."

"Well, generally so," she admitted. "But other lands have other ideas."

"We're talking about the US of A."

"We are? I didn't know that," she teased. "But go on."

116

"Okay, then go back centuries ago—in Rome it was right to kill slaves in Roman games to put Christians in the Arena. Go ahead in time and you'll find more changes."

"Yes, of course, go ahead, into the distant future where no man has gone before!"

"Hey...are you a Trekkie?"

"Well, once in my youth," she admitted, laughing.

That stopped Hank.

"I'm sorry, Bobbie. I didn't mean to get so excited. Normally I don't spout off like that. Maybe it's because I'm trying to find a sane answer to my own life and find my own direction."

He looked at her, and felt the emotion welling through him—the need to make her understand exactly how he felt.

"I'm making an ass out of myself!"

"No, not really." Then she laughing said: "No more than any man does."

"That's not fair!"

"Sure it is. All's fair in love and war...well, okay, sorry. Didn't mean to suggest...oh, now you got me going!" She looked away, avoiding his eyes.

She looked so desperate. Lost. Like a little girl.

He wanted to comfort her. And throw his arms around her and just embrace her whole being in his. Instead he sat there like a fool kid in heat, helpless in front of the first girl he had fallen in love with.

You're a fool, he thought. *A damned fool!*

To break the long silence that smothered down on them, he started speaking nervously, picking up his earlier theme: "What's really right and wrong? I don't believe anybody has all the answers, yet. Even the Bible creates confusion."

"Really, now?" She sounded fully recovered and re-engaged.

"Well, you have to admit—"

"No I don't!" she shook her head. "Don't have to admit to anything!"

"You have to admit, even assuming that the Bible was revealed to the men who wrote it—that it is in human symbols, and human symbols aren't perfect in explaining or expressing complex ideas in a way that enables everyone to understand them in just the same way. Every person who reads the Bible has a different interpretation of the words, even if they're taken literally. Words are words. Symbols which project a thought image in the mind of a person."

"You don't have to tell me anything about words. That's my business."

"So I heard."

"Well, go on. Please. I'm truly interested."

He gave her a double look, and was surprised to see real interest in her eyes. "Okay. Nothing can be judged as right or wrong except what you believe is right or wrong within yourself. What I might feel for you or want—"

Hank broke off. Suddenly Bobbie was laughing, doubled over in throbbing convulsions of mirth.

For a moment, anger threatened to burst through Hank; then as she looked up he saw the open honesty and frankness sparkling in her eyes, and he couldn't help laughing, too. Suddenly he didn't care. He just wanted to take her into his arms, cover her lips, explore the pent up emotions which gathered inside him.

So he just laughed.

Finally Bobbie gained control of herself and said, "I'm sorry. You were so serious. Well, I couldn't help myself."

"I'm sorry too. I shouldn't spout off—"

"No. I'm glad you did," Bobbie said. "You made some interesting points. Maybe you're right that we should grab hold of life, reach out for what we want and be willing to fight for it. I'll have to do a lot of thinking about that."

"What's there to think about?" he asked. "I'm right, of course. And everybody else is wrong!"

She shook her head, then asked: "But if there's no real right or wrong, what's to keep a person in line—keep them from just letting their animal passions take over? What code of ethics should a person live by?"

Hank considered said: "I guess the way to live is to do as much good for others as possible. To make the happiest life you can for yourself and those around you. To do

118

nothing that would hurt another human being—"

"I mean, what about morality?"

"Morality? Well, I've always believed that what two consenting adults do is their own business. As long as they don't hurt anybody other than themselves."

Bobbie nodded and was silent for a long time. Then she looked up and asked for another cigarette.

"I don't know what got us started on all that." Then to change the subject, he offered: "You say you write?"

"For women's magazines. The net, too. Women's issues. Purely a hobby. Sold about a dozen stories in the last five years; I do it part time."

"Pay much?"

"Enough to take me on a couple of vacations a year," Bobbie told him. "What do you do?"

"A little of everything. I'm looking for something now. I was in Hollywood a few years, made a little money producing movies. Los Cheapos, Deluxe! Fast production, on limited budgets with professionals—who were underpaid, natch! Quickie flicks with good profits. But...not artistically thrilling! No commercial Big Bucks."

"Oh?" Her voice showed interest.

"Not anymore. Couldn't take the rat race. Want to live a quiet life, now." He had told the truth, even if a bit slanted to sound more impressive than depressive. X-rated films were hardly prize things one bragged about. That had, of course, been limited. And didn't need to be openly admitted to.

She asked: "Ever try writing?"

"Not really."

"Never can tell. With your ability to spout off, you should be able to develop it into a good writing style. If you wanted to work at it."

"I don't know what I want to do. All my life I've been struggling and trying to find a means of survival. That can be a harsh master! Just surviving is a prime objective at which all too many people fail. I've done pretty well at times. Guess my best talent is the ability to promote."

"A professional con man?" Bobbie asked, smiling. "That sounds illegal."

"No. That's not the way I meant it."

She laughed. Hank looked at his watch. It had been well over an hour and a half since the others had left them. Maybe another hour would pass before rescue came. He hoped the helicopter would arrive before the storm really broke into full force.

"Well," she commented, thoughtfully, "might be an interesting place for a young writer to make a score."

"What?"

"Hollywood. Difficult to get into films?"

"As what?"

"A writer, I suppose."

"Thank God. I was worried you wanted to become an actress."

"Heaven forbid. Why that?"

"Well, you're certainly good looking enough."

"Oh, yeah, compliments. They could get you any-where."

"I wonder."

"At least that'll keep you out of trouble. Wondering." He shrugged.

"Well?" she asked, again, "about writing scripts?"

"You want to do that?"

"I've toyed with it."

"Damn hard to get in. If you haven't sold one, you can't get an agent or get any producer to look at your work, unless you know somebody. Dead end there."

"Really that hard?"

"Really."

"I know 'you'!" she laughed. "Wouldn't you help a girl in desperate need?"

"That sounds just like a starlet I know…in fact a lot of starlets I've known."

"Is that really so bad?"

"Well, very…if you want the truth. The Casting Couch is alive and well."

"I thought that was illegal now days."

"Sure. Of course it is. But what happens between men and women in private, consenting adults and all that…well, quite frankly anything goes. And goes!"

120

"Depressing thought," she noted. "Talent should win out."

"It does. The trouble is that talent is cheap! And everybody wants in! And there are just so many openings. And, well, if you don't have the connections, don't have the ambition and drive strong enough, if you don't stick it out, and most of all have right timing and bloody good luck, you might as well bat your head against a stone wall!"

"Don't like stone walls, thank you."

They sat there for a long time, not speaking, still wrapped in their own thoughts.

He sat there feeling slightly uncomfortable, remembering a bit why he'd wanted to get away from Hollywood for a few weeks. The life could be depressive. Some of the women he'd met in the film business were all too willing to do anything for a few bucks, for a fix, for just a chance to do a film—to make it up one more rung on the Hollywood ladder. That life could be really tough on young women. And some literally fell through the cracks into the porno industry or onto the streets as prostitutes. Some got lucky and elevated themselves into escort services, even getting successful enough to consider themselves high-priced call-girls. But it was all the same. If they didn't make it in films they got routine jobs 9-5 or ended up on the streets. Ugly business. And he'd seen enough of that to turn him cold. It wasn't the kind of life he wanted. Even on the fringes. His connection with the porno thing was short and not-so-sweet, regardless of a couple of rather nicely hot women who were desperate enough to do whatever was necessary to please a "producer" or "investor". One lady had become highly successful in making sex films and wanted so desperately to go legit that she'd literally begged him to give her a break, saying she would do anything to make it worth his wife. And she sure, as hell, did. For a long weekend she'd taken him around the world and back, then out into deep orbit so wild that it had left him dazed and exhausted. As delightful an experience as it was, there had been one basic quality missing; actual caring, feeling, emotion. The woman had all the skills down pat, but no sense of emotional caring. That experienced had soured him completely. He simply wanted out. A seedy busi-

121

ness at best. Even if, now, somewhat legal. That's why he'd stepped out of that racket. Films, even cheapies, as long as they were legit could be iffy—even for the smart operators. He'd been lucky. If one wanted to call it that.

Then a new sound broke over the noise of the racing wind, and the body of a helicopter slowly edged down from the skies, coming to rest at the entrance of the cave.

Hank stood and helped Bobbie to her feet.

"I hope you'll forget my earlier rudeness," Bobbie said, her hand reaching out instinctively toward him.

"About what?"

"We are friends, then?"

"Naturally." Hank laughed, taking her hand and moving toward the helicopter. "The best of friends, I hope."

Bobbie's fingers squeezed his and that implied meaning sent a stab of excitement through him.

Then the copter door opened and they were swiftly helped on board.

Chapter Four

Hank had been in his cabin a little less than an hour, lying on his bed, thinking about Bobbie Lee and the way she made him feel, when there was a soft knock on the door. For a moment he couldn't clear from his mind the boyish female form which had been so vividly present there.

The knocking repeated.

"Who is it?"

"Vicky," said a low sensual voice.

"Be right there." He got up, opened the door, then closed it behind Vicky López.

"Well, to what do I owe this visit?" Puzzled, Hank walked over to the dresser, where he had a bottle of whiskey and a couple of glasses.

"García will be here tomorrow," Vicky reminded him in a sultry voice. "I thought you'd—we could enjoy some time together!"

Hank turned and looked at her.

After the hours he had spent with Bobbie Lee, Vicky seemed strangely coarse and crude. Common. The darkness of her olive skin and the jet black of her long flowing hair only seemed to accent her sensuality. His eyes flowed over her figure. She was a hot Latin-cat who had burning fire for blood, raw lust for eyes, and lava heat for flesh.

But what else? Nothing?

She wasn't Bobbie Lee, and his guts were burning for that woman. Bobbie was the kind of lady a man had to take very seriously.

"Strange," he muttered, half to himself.

"What?"

That shook him out of the sudden daze. "I don't even

know."

"You worried about García?" she quickly inquired.

"Heck, who knows?" He shrugged that off. "Okay, maybe. A little."

"Don't!" she quickly responded. "García's just a rich man with hunger for pretty things. He's demanding—but a poor lover. I'm his girl, for what I can get from him."

Her honesty amazed him. It was somewhat charming, too. "And what's that?"

His eyes were now taking in her sensual beauty, drinking in the curves, remembering how she'd felt draped hungrily around him. She was all hot surrender.

"Money and trinkets. Nothing more. He buys me things, and I let him amuse himself!" Vicky answered in a low, bitter voice.

Hank nodded, then took a sip of his drink.

"Aren't you going to offer me a drink?" Vicky asked.

"Help yourself!"

She shrugged and glided across the room. Her hip brushed his as she came to a stop before the dresser and reached for a glass. She poured several inches of whiskey, then turned and looked invitingly at him. "What's gotten into you?"

"What do you mean?" Hank was uneasy.

"You're different from this morning."

"This is now."

"That's no answer," Vicky countered good-naturedly, taking a gulp of her drink.

"That'll have to do." Hank was more irritated with himself than with Vicky.

She was silent, then laughed nervously. "I bet I know what happened."

"What?"

"You and Miss Lee."

"Bull!" Hank cursed, walking angrily toward her. "Not all women are whores!"

She looked challengingly at him, unflinching. The implication of his words had no outward effect on her.

Hank's hands clamped on Vicky's shoulders. He squeezed them. Hard.

124

Vicky laughed.

"Hit a sore spot?" she teased, looking mockingly at him. "She's not putting out for a guy. Not like I do. Right?"

For a moment he stood there, clutching her shoulders.

Bobbie had gone to her room for the night, tired and drained by the day's experience. And he wanted her so much it hurt.

Hank finally relaxed completely. "No. She's different!"

"And me?" she mocked.

"You're the one who came here!" Hank pointed out.

"Maybe you're right." Vicky paused to sip her drink, then added: "And you're just like me. Admit it. We enjoy! For the moment. Take what is offered. Drown in the pleasures."

He merely stared at her.

"You're like me, Hank, because I don't demand anything from you but what we can do...at the moment. Instant escape."

He wanted to argue that point, but couldn't. She was right. Instead he walked over to the bed and lay down, looking at the ceiling. He almost hated himself for wanting this woman in such a low down animal way.

"Don't kid me," Vicky snapped, gulping more whiskey. "Find a woman that won't let you play her like an organ grinder and you start getting respectable."

Hank felt sorry for his attitude. "Oh, don't be silly."

He patted the bed. "Just say I was tired from the hike. Leave it there."

Vicky downed the rest of her drink and walked slowly to the bed. She slid down next to him, caressing his chest.

"You know, it's a damned shame that García is here tomorrow. We could sure have had a ball!"

"Does he have to know everything?"

"If you knew García, like I know García, oh, oh, oh, what a growl!" She laughed at that. "He's known to be nasty. But...never you worry about that, honey. I'm all closed mouth."

"I hope not tonight."

125

"Well, not here and now, I promise! But from tomorrow on ...you don't need to tangle with him."

"I can take care of myself," Hank assured her.

"So can García. And he usually has help at his right and left hands."

Hank let his hand rest on her shoulder, gently, now—caressing.

Hank reached for her, and she came easily into his arms.

Time blurred.

There was a soft, timid knock on the door. Hank didn't hear it at first. The knock sounded again.

He stood groggily and moved from the bed. "Who is it?"

"Bobbie," a soft voice answered.

Shock jolted through him. What was Bobbie doing here?

"Yes?"

"Can I come in?"

"What do you want?"

"Well, I thought we were friends. Do I need a reason?" Hank thought he detected tension in her words, but he couldn't be sure.

He turned and looked at the half conscious Vicky lying totally naked on the bed. He groaned inwardly.

Bobbie's voice was tight now. "You have someone in there? Can't I come in?"

"I'm not decent."

Frantically he tried to think of some way to get rid of either Vicky or Bobbie without ruining things.

Bobbie's reply was soft, hesitant. "I don't really mind."

The implication was blunt enough.

Hank looked once more at Vicky, who was now sitting up in bed gazing questioningly at him. She smiled as his eyes met hers.

Desperately he shook his head, indicating she shouldn't make a sound.

Hank knew there wasn't anything he could do but send Bobbie Lee away. Damning himself, he turned back to

126

the door.

But what difference should it make? He thought bitterly. *He had all the women he needed.*

"I'm sorry, Bobbie. I can't."

"Well...if you say so," was her comment, small, a bit disappointed, even a shade angry and hurt. "See you, I suppose."

"Sorry. Really."

He was sure he heard a muffled "shit" come from the other side of the door. Footsteps sound, faded.

Hank turned, facing Vicky. She sat there, naked, arms reaching out for him.

"Come and cry on Mommy's shoulders," she offered softly, the expression on her face revealing she'd read the situation correctly. "I'll wipe your tears away with hot kisses, and you'll just get lost in the wonderful joy of my comforting embrace. I promise. I'll be good. Real good and nice for the hurt little boy!"

The way she said all that was charming, even cutting through the hurt. And there was no way to avoid the automatic response of his body at the sight of her voluptuous form.

She smiled, winking. "I do think you're fully prepared for a second go around!"

Then in order to totally snap his mind to the present she said: "Just for now, honey. I'm all yours!"

He moved down to her and took her into his arms. His embrace was demanding.

"Oh," she murmured, "such a strong beastie, you are! Going to ravish me, jungle style?"

He laughed, but angrily forced himself to forget Bobbie. There wasn't anything he could do about that. But he could take Vicky's generously offered body.

She shuddered happily as his lips covered hers. Their tongues meet fiercely as she melted into his mood as well as into his arms. In moments they were stretched out on the bed, locked savagely together, gasping at every movement driving them at one another with almost brutal force. And he was lost in the pleasure of her, lost in the wild sensations that bathed over his flesh at every point of contact. She devoured all of him with such greedy intent that his mind was aware of nothing else.

Later, when he regained consciousness, he was alone.

Chapter Five

Laying there in bed, he ran his mind back and forth across the entire day, from Vicky to Bobbie, then Vicky again.

There was no doubt that Vicky had been good to him. But she wasn't Bobbie. And, more importantly, whatever they had shared, it was now over. Finished.

All he could think of was Bobbie Lee. He didn't try to reason it out. Even with a couple of drinks, it was a very long time before sleep finally faded over his troubled thoughts.

Hank awakened with the desert in his mouth. He felt dragged out and exhausted, unable to move. The effects of Vicky López' demanding passions still strained his nerves. At least she'd served a wonderful purpose in that department.

Finally he sat up in bed.

Slowly he moved to the bathroom. He needed a shower, then maybe he'd feel better.

Afterwards he fixed himself a strong drink and downed it. The liquor burned his throat and then settled in his stomach. For several seconds he stood, letting the effects soothe through him.

Hank grimaced.

Then found his thoughts once again centering on Bobbie, wondering why he had been so instantly attracted to her. That wasn't his normal style. And he certainly wasn't in any desperate need for a woman—Vicky had satisfied those needs. Any woman could do that to some degree.

But his quick fascination for Bobbie Lee was haunting. Why? Somehow it seemed as if he'd known her for a very long time.

His thoughts played with that, and even in the dumb daze of the hangover he suddenly realize the truth. It hit him like a hard hammer.

It was Bobbie Lee.

When he was in the hospital recovering from the auto accident—caring for his shattered leg—he'd met a nurse very much like Bobbie. It was his first real romance. And it all happened in Germany before he was carted back to the States and discharged. He had planned on returning to Germany to get her, but it never worked out that way. Apparently he'd been more involved with her than she with him.

Now Hank realized what it was about Bobbie Lee that so strongly attracted him. He hadn't thought about the nurse until just now—she had simply been forced down in a deep slot of his mind and left there to churn silently away as a fading event overtaken by the routine act of simply surviving from day to day, year to year.

Hank took another drink and then moved to the door. As he stepped out of the cabin, the hot sun blazed down upon him. For a moment he was tempted to return to his cabin and get drunk, then he changed his mind. He was drinking too much, anyway.

He went to the coffee shop, ordered breakfast and ate. Twenty minutes later he walked out to stand in front of the lodge. The urge to find Bobbie Lee edged through him, but he forced it down. Instead, he decided to take a walk.

The sun was hotter than before and it burned down on him with fiery fingers. If it weren't for the red, welts on his back which Vicky's fingernails had drawn the night before, he might have gone swimming. He turned toward the small lake a little way from the Lodge. This was a lovely small resort where he'd come several times in the past. His private escape set in a small valley cut into the mountains. But this morning these visual wonders were no more than a blurred background to his troubled mind.

Jumbled thoughts twisted up inside him with every step he took. There was something happening to him inside, which he couldn't quite figure out. During the last couple of days an inward tension had been building up within him

130

which was gradually being sparked to a raging flame. Raging and unreasonable.

Hank shook his head slowly from side to side and forced his eyes to focus on his surroundings. He was standing at the edge of the small blue lake. The sandy shores were dotted with sunning people; the cool waters were filled with happy swimmers.

Again, he forced his thoughts away from himself. His eyes moved along the shoreline and then suddenly came to rest on a young woman in a white bikini who was lying on the sand. For a moment he was more struck by her figure than anything else. Then he recognized the shape and form.

Bobbie Lee.

Without realizing it he was automatically almost rushing towards her. He came to a stop just a few feet away from her.

Without thinking, he said: "Hello."

It took several seconds before he received a reply or reaction from Bobbie. She lay there, not moving.

Then she stirred, and her eyes opened.

"Go away," she ordered in a soft, even voice. Her eyes snapped shut again.

For a long time Hank stood there, taking in the loveliness of her. She had a trim figure; hips that were slightly narrowed, but rounded and enticing. Her figure wasn't gigantic like Vicky's, but more softly feminine.

"Bobbie—about last night..."

"Don't explain to me," she told him. The angry words came out choppy, stabbing.

"That's not it."

Bobbie suddenly sat up, opened her eyes and looked directly into his. There was a sadness, a wounded doe look, in her expression. But her words were bitter and sharp.

"Then what is it?"

"I thought we were supposed to be friends," Hank said. Bobbie nervously bit her lower lip, but her eyes didn't leave his for even a moment. "That's what I thought, last night. But..." she shrugged, looked away.

"Damn it all, Bobbie."

Her eyes snapped back to him, saying it all. There

was anger and hurt mixed with a silent statement that he could hardly say anything that would explain it all away.

"Do you expect me to go around blind?" He felt like a damned fool. Angry, defensive.

"Doesn't matter." Her tense body revealed that to be an outright lie.

"What did you expect?"

"Not much. Not that, apparently. And…well, so you were with another woman. I guess that's your right."

"Damn right it is!"

"So…stop trying to explain things to me! I'm not interested, really." That last was said almost as an incomplete statement, her eyes silently finished it, *not any more!*

"You weren't even in the offering—" He broke off, realizing this wasn't the kind of thing Bobbie Lee would consider flattering. Immediately he wanted to withdraw the words.

"That's what I mean!" she cried. "I almost believed you were different. You give out a beautiful line. Do you create it for the moment? Well, I'm not the kind of girl who goes for all that. So, no thanks! No way."

"Then what do you…go for?" Hank blurted out, frustrated, damning himself for having said all the wrong things.

"Obviously not…you!" she snapped, glaring up at him.

"Hell, what does it take—?"

Bobbie's eyes dropped. "Just leave me alone! Will you? Please? Just stop bothering me! I have better things to do!"

She lifted her head and glared at him.

"What? This is a vacation place. I figure you're here to have some fun and…" Again the words were all wrong.

"You don't know the meaning of fun!" she snapped. "Oh, go away!"

"Bobbie, please." He was desperate to make her understand. "So there *was* someone with me—I'll admit that—but it wasn't what you thought." He broke off, feeling stupid about the lie.

"What do you think I thought?" she suddenly offered, tiredly, "What could I think."

132

Then he blurted: "Why am I bothering?"

"Right. Why bother...me? Just go away. Get somebody who'll...does...whatever! Quite frankly, mister swinger, stud-man, whatever you call yourself, I'm not interested in playing your kind of game. Find somebody else to take up your time and leave me alone! Is that clear enough?"

"Too clear, if you ask me!" He was furious and even angrier because she made him care so much.

"Go. Go!" She slapped her hands together with each word, as if smacking an annoying fly. "Just go, go, go. Away!"

He started down at her, wanting to both sweep the woman into his arms and at the same time smack her across that smug face of hers.

"Oh, to hell with it!"

Hank turned and walked back toward his cabin. Now the confusion was more terrible than ever before. He needed a drink, right then, more than anything in the world. Something to soothe away the churning anger inside him. He had never been so fired up by any woman before in this manner! And he hardly even knew her! In fact he hadn't allowed himself to be bothered by a woman for a long time—not since the little Hollywood starlet who had suckered him into marriage. Women like Vicky had filled in for any real relationship. None quite like Vicky, actually, 'cause she was, in fact, above average, one hell of a fun time lady. He didn't need somebody like Bobbie Lee in his life. And, quite obviously she wasn't interested in him.

He made his way to the Lodge and into the bar. He sat on a stool and ordered a double martini. A couple of quick jolts and he'd return to his cabin.

He was cursing inwardly as he slammed the door of his cabin behind him. He didn't notice the two men waiting for him.

Hands grabbed Hank; a pair of fists smashed into his body before he could do anything but feel the pain of the impact. It all happened so fast that he didn't even see the men's faces.

"Keep away from her!" a raspy voice snarled as a knee slammed up into his groin. "Hands off!"

Nausea ripped through Hank like a painful, agonizing, clawing hand.

Another fist hit his face.

One more into his stomach, then a rabbit punch slammed the back of his head, putting out the lights. The last thing he remembered was caressing the floor.

Chapter Six

It was like swimming on a lake, black with night. It seemed to last for a long while, as if all the world and all the universe had decided to suspend time while he tried to think his way out of the maze that had enveloped his brain.

Then images formed in the dark of his mind. There was the olive cream of female flesh—then he remembered the name that went with it: Vicky López.

Why was he thinking of her? He had to find the answer to that before he would be back to the world of reality.

García Flynn! A fat, ugly, evil man.

García Flynn! Hank's mind roared.

Light burst into his eyes. He found himself in the front room of his cabin, staring up into blinding light.

It was several seconds before any other sensation came to him. The first was awareness of pain. His body ached, and the back of his neck hurt. The next pain was between his legs; numb now, but a grim reminder of the brutal blow which had been placed there.

Then anger flared, mixed with nausea rippling hot through his body.

That son-of-a-bitch-bastard! He cursed, struggling to stand.

Angry pains stabbed through him as he came slowly to his feet. Staggering over to his dresser, Hank took the bottle of whiskey in his large hands. After pulling off the top, he gulped from its neck until he felt the effects of the liquor hit his stomach and flood through his body. Then he stood there, dazedly looking at the far wall, feeling the sensations rush through his body and mind.

Anger. Hate. Disgust. They became a reality, pulsing

135

like insanity through him.

He staggered toward his bed and stood there, swaying again.

Suddenly he knew what must be done!

He turned towards the door, opened it.

As he stepped outside he was stopped short at the sight of Bobbie Lee walking up. For a long stunned moment he stared at her, unable to adjust to this new development. The anger and hate that had possessed him now changed, gently fading.

He didn't know what to say to her. Finally he managed a weak, uncertain "Hello."

She quickly spoke, fast, as if verbalizing thoughts: "I wanted to tell you—well, I acted like a little bitch!"

She broke off upon seeing his face, startled. "What happened to you?"

"Nothing." He didn't want to tell her anything about that.

"Something happened," she insisted, reaching an instinctive hand toward his face. "You look like a banged up prize fighter! You in trouble?"

Hank nodded, helpless to know what to say. There was an embarrassed silence. He wanted to get lost in her arms. He wanted her to leave. It always seemed that Bobbie turned up at the wrong time.

Hank suddenly noticed how attractively Bobbie was dressed. She wore a white blouse and a tight-fitting dark gray skirt. The clothes accented her slender shape, giving it an intriguing attractiveness. Her brown eyes gazed up at him, wide and doe-like, as if staring right into his soul. He was torn between need for revenge, and a haunting desire for her.

"What can I do for you?" Hank finally managed.

"Just wanted to tell you...but isn't there something I can do for your face?"

"Nothing." He shrugged helplessly. "I'll live."

"I wanted to say I'm sorry. I've been...it was childish, foolish. After all, we're adults, and why should I think we should be—" Bobbie hesitated, then said after a moment, "Well, I hope we can be...friends?"

Hank was confused. The word "friends" had become

136

a battleground between them.

"Men and women aren't just friends!" he said a little harshly. "If that's the only way you want it, then—"

"That's not what I meant!" Bobbie's voice seemed embarrassed, almost shy. She lowered her eyes for a moment.

He decided to bring things to a head. The game they were playing was impossible. A rotten dance of lies. "Then come on in. I have something to take care of, but I'll be right back. You can help yourself to a drink if you want."

Bobbie hesitated only for a moment, then nodded and stepped into the cabin. "Will you be long?"

"A few minutes," Hank promised. Without another word he turned and started down the path toward the Lodge.

Walking into the lobby, he moved to the desk clerk. "Do you know if García Flynn is in?"

The clerk looked up. "I saw him walk through the lobby toward the cocktail lounge. Miss López was with him."

Hank turned. The moment he stepped into the cocktail lounge he spotted Vicky López. She was sitting alone in a booth.

He approached the table.

"Vicky—"

"Go away!" she snapped. "Split, before García finds you here." There was raw fear in her voice. Her eyes widened as she saw his face. Open concern and fear distorted her features.

"Where is he?" Hank demanded coldly.

"Just split—fast! Forget me! It won't do any good."

"What won't it do any good?" A heavy, dangerous voice sounded from behind him.

Hank whipped around, facing the heavy-set man. Their eyes locked.

García's voice was dangerously silky. "So you're the stud-man."

"What's that make you?" Hank retorted, angrily aware that he didn't know exactly what to do next.

"Hank, please," Vicky pleaded, rising from her seat and extending her hands toward him. "It's no good."

137

"Let him dig a grave," García suggested sweetly in a controlled voice. He glared at Hank again, his face turning cold and hard. "If I were you, sonny, I'd chill out. You were lucky. Accept my little lesson in manners. I let you off, easy, this time. It was cheap."

The man's contemptuous and icy voice settled it. Those eyes dismissed him, as if a hand had waved him away.

Without conscious decision, Hank plunged his right fist straight into the man's gut. He followed that with a powerful swing to García's jaw, then sliced the side of his hand into the man's throat.

García turned pasty white, his face distorting in agony, staring at Hank. Tears welled up in the man's eyes, which suddenly closed. With a horrid gasp, his body collapsed to the floor.

"Sorry," Hank threw at Vicky.

It was then that cold sweat broke out on Hank's forehead. Stunned, he moved from the cocktail lounge, stepped into the evening and took a deep breath of clear air.

For a long time he stood there, numbed at what he had done.

He must be mad!

Confused thoughts rushed through his brain. It had been a damned foolish and dangerous thing to do. Perhaps he had deserved the working over García's boys had given him. That really didn't matter.

Hank slowly walked to his cabin. He opened the door and stepped inside.

"Hello again," a female voice brightly greeted him.

Hank jumped. He had forgotten all about Bobbie. He stared at her boyish figure curled up on the sofa. She was sipping a highball, gazing at him over the rim of the glass. She had a wide, innocent look about her that was beautifully refreshing. She lowered the glass; the expression on her lips was haunting—a seductive offering.

"Well, what's wrong?" she asked, taking another sip of her drink. "Why not join me?"

Hank stepped over to the table where Bobbie Lee had put the bottle of whiskey. He poured a shot, downed it. His insides warmed almost immediately. The warmth grew, then

138

reached his head.

"What're you doing? Having a party all your own?" Bobbie's voice was bright.

Hank stared at her, puzzled. She was a strange woman. Impossible to outguess. He'd never met anybody quite like her.

The top of Bobbie's blouse was unbuttoned, parted a little, and he could see the edge of her lazy white bra. There was an open, brazen brightness in her eyes. Determined.

He stood there, staring, trying to figure the woman out. Then he swallowed more whiskey and moved to the door, bolting it. He turned toward Bobbie.

This was a woman who could inspire feelings he hadn't experienced for years.

It couldn't be love. Love was something that took time to grow. Yet it couldn't be anything short of it.

"You look like a frightened little boy!" Bobbie teased. "I won't run away. I couldn't anyhow; this ankle is still sore."

With an almost ironic sense of pleasure, Hank realized she was referring to his act of bolting the door.

Without answering he moved to the sofa and sat down beside her.

"Nothing like that," he assured her.

It seemed to *him* that they were playing through a movie scene, rather than acting out real life. Maybe the whiskey made him feel that way. He didn't know. But everything seemed unreal. Yet there was no doubt about the reality of her sitting there beside him, nor its implications.

Looking directly into those lovely brown eyes, he felt that strange emotion choke up through him once more. "Exactly what kind of beautiful witch are you? What magic spell have you cast over me?"

"What kind do you want?" she countered, finishing her drink and handing over the empty glass. "Another, please."

Silently Hank walked to the table, picked up the bottle and returned to the sofa, this time sitting closer to Bobbie. He filled the glass, and placed the bottle on the floor. He put his arm around Bobby and gently pulled her to him.

"I don't know exactly what to think about you. You puzzle me. One moment you're running cold and then this..." He hesitated, thinking, then continued. "Are you the kind of lovely lady who fights her honest emotions, and after deciding to stop resisting becomes a temptress who draws men to their doom?"

She leaned closer, her lips half parting. Her arms began to slide around his neck.

Then the closeness of her, the warmth of her breath on his cheek, drove away all thoughts and questions. Only desire remained.

Hank pulled her tiny form to his, covering her lips. There was warmth, delightful softness, tenderness, in the first kiss. The buzz in his head began to grow louder as his heart pounded wildly. He felt surrounded with love, caressed in a tide of romantic wine which cleaned his soul with a perfection of golden light. It raised him upward into a heaven of ecstasy—spiritual ecstasy that far surpassed anything so common place as mere physical desire.

The rapture of her embrace left his whole body fired with more than passion. He had never felt this way—not even with the nurse of whom she had reminded him.

Hank was deliciously conscious of the contact of her form. It wonderfully numbed all thoughts of Vicky and García, of the outside world.

He wasn't even aware of the physical actions of making love to her. Not in details. It was a blur of feelings, sensations, a dive into an endless well, which simply swallowed him up.

He only knew a sense of her soft, yielding flesh that seemed to surround him from every side. He was aware of having touched, caressed, kissed her breasts; aware of the sensations; aware of exploring her total body. It was more than physical ecstasy; it was a soul shattering merging. It felt as if the two of them had become one unified creature, rather than two separate bodies slamming out sexual pleasure with one another. It wasn't merely a biological mating, but something that reached deeper within him: a blending together that left only the perfection of two souls joined in peaceful oneness. And this was love in the highest sense.

140

Hank knew then that there could be no experience like this with another woman. Only with Bobbie Lee could he ever enjoy such completeness.

<u>Chapter Seven</u>

Hank lay in bed for a long time after he awakened. There was a strange sense of well being. He couldn't shake it off, and he had the feeling that he should shake it off.

He was doing a lot of thinking about himself, and about his past and future. But he found no answers.

Ever since childhood he'd been running from one thing to another like a man with a thorn in his hide. Nothing had kept his attention for long—only until he'd proven that it could be done. Once something was worked out, resolved, set up, he had moved on to some new project; not looking back. So where had it led him? Nowhere!

Hank felt movement beside him, and turned. Bobbie Lee was still sleeping. The childlike, innocent look about her face made him think back to those moments, long and wonderful, in her arms the evening before. And with that thought came feelings and emotions which hadn't bothered him for years; emotions that were somewhat frightening.

She had given so completely—pleasure, affection. As if a damn had been brushed away somewhere in her mind and now, once in his arms, she offered all of herself, freely offering everything there was for a woman to give.

That thought jolted Hank. He found himself wondering why she had given so fully, so completely.

"Say, what're you doing?" Bobbie's sleepy voice asked.

Hank turned and looked down at her. "Sorry. I was shut up in my mind."

"Oh?"

"Thinking, I guess."

"In the morning?" Bobbie complained, frowning and

143

sitting up in bed. "With a woman beside you?"

"You were sleeping."

Bobbie grinned and slid her arms around his neck. "I'm not sleeping any more."

Hank pulled her to him and covered her lips gently with his, marveling at the silky softness of her mouth.

Bobbie shivered and then teasingly pushed away. "That's not very nice."

"You like it?"

"Sure," she smiled, then added: "What are we going to do about ourselves?"

"I don't know," he answered honestly. "I just don't know. Nobody ever hit me like you have. It's almost weird. Something you can't touch, can't see or understand, but you can feel. When I met you the first evening, and you iced it off, I...I don't know what happened, but something drew me to you—something I didn't understand then, and I don't understand now."

Bobbie nodded. "Yes. I know. There was something. I felt it, too. Something that fired between us." She smiled. "You don't know how much it upset me. That night I went back to my cabin and just lay on the bed, thinking, wondering. It was like being hit with a soft—hammer?" She laughed throatily, her eyes gleaming.

"Then why—why the icy treatment?" he demanded, startled.

"Oh, I'd...been involved with a...well, a rat, quite frankly, not too long ago. I simply didn't want to start something down right foolish. And maybe get hurt. And I was bitter. Afraid, I guess. A person gets afraid of being hurt. And you run away from it—fast! I saw hurt, or thought I saw hurt, when I looked at you. Maybe I was right, but I don't care any more. You have to grab life and fight with it. You were right about that. I want love, just like any other normal girl, but... So, where now? A summer romance, or what?"

Hank shook his head thoughtfully. "I don't think so. I don't know." He felt a sudden nagging depression.

After a long silence, Bobby said, "Maybe it's too soon to know what we've gotten ourselves into."

"I guess you're right," Hank admitted. He sat up and

144

looked at the far wall, thinking, trying to sort out his emotions and feelings so that he could understand them.

He wasn't aware that Bobbie had slipped out of bed until he heard her movement in the shower. Hank sat for some time, thinking, then stood and went to the small kitchenette, reaching for the bottle of whiskey on the sink.

He was pouring himself a shot when he realized he didn't really want a drink.

Why am I doing this, then? He puzzled. *Habit?*

Hank was startled, for the habit was broken. Boozing suddenly wasn't desirable any more. It meant little but escape, and suddenly he realized that escape wasn't what he wanted now. Instead, he wanted to remain sober, to take in every moment with every awareness in him. To experience fully every sight, every breath, every word, every feeling. And although he didn't completely understand it, he knew the reason.

Bobbie Lee!

He wanted to feel and breathe and taste her nearness, fully alert, fully aware.

Bobbie Lee stepped out of the bathroom, a towel wrapped around her body. She stood there looking at him, bright excitement in her eyes. At that moment she seemed to Hank the loveliest thing in the world.

He approached her and tenderly took her into his arms.

Just then there was a knock on the front door. For a moment he ignored it.

"Hank, are you there?" called Vicky's voice. "Hank! This is important. Hank! Please. If you're there, for God's sake answer me."

Bobbie tensed; her eyes flashed fiery emotion.

"Please, Bobbie," Hank pleaded. "She doesn't mean a damn to me."

Her silence was cold and brutalizing.

Hank stood tensely, undecided.

Vicky called again. "It's life and death! Please, Hank, if you're there."

He decided.

"Yes!" he called, fairly pushing Bobbie into the other

145

room, closing the door. He pulled on his pants and crossed to the other door and let Vicky in.

She rushed forward, her face distorted in fear. On her cheek was an ugly purple bruise.

"What's happened?"

"Don't ask questions, for God's sake," Vicky pleaded. "Don't ask questions!"

At that point there were footsteps outside, and before Hank could react or move, the door was flung violently open.

Two men stood there.

"What the goddamned hell!" Hank blurted.

One of the men moved his hand to his coat and pulled out a .38 revolver.

"Just stay put, and don't try anything!" he ordered, motioning Hank to step back against the far wall as he moved forward.

"You too, Miss López. Good thing the boss had us keep an eye on you. He thought something like this might happen."

Hank felt panic rush through him, then forced the feeling down. He had to think clearly. Bobbie Lee was in the other room. As long as they didn't know about it, there was a chance she might be able to slip out the back window, get away and find some help. He prayed silently that this would be what she'd do.

"Where're you taking us?" he demanded, not moving.

"Nowhere," the taller of the two said. "Jake, go get García!"

When the other had left, Hank turned to Vicky. "What is this all about?"

Vicky's face was tense, her eyes wide with terror, her lips white rimmed. "García threatened to have you really worked over if I didn't do something for him. He's been after me for weeks. García's a dirty little man, in the dirty business of blackmail." She hesitated, swallowed, and lowered her eyes.

"I'm sorry about this, Hank. I didn't mean to get you involved. It has nothing to do with you—just that you hap-

146

pened to be around, and García saw a way to push me into line. I just couldn't do what he asked. A girl will just go so far. He wanted too much."

"I don't get it," was all he could say.

"García wanted me to sleep with a man so he could get pictures of it—he wanted to blackmail the guy for a big wad. I couldn't do it. I had refused some days ago. Last night when he recovered from your attack he was furious. He would have had you killed immediately. The only thing I could do was stall for time. I told him I'd sleep with his sucker if he'd just leave you alone.

"Last night I figured I'd try to get away, and warn you to get out of here before it was too late. This morning I got my chance."

She broke off, her voice filled with defeat and bitterness. "Some chance!"

The man continued to hold the gun on them, and grinned. "You think too much for a dumb broad. You should've played along, and everything would have gone smoothly. Now you've fixed things up real tight. Now your boy here will get what's coming to him."

Hank was still stunned, finding it hard to believe this was happening. His thoughts raced, and suddenly everything seemed to jell, to fit together and form a pattern. Strangely, the pattern had nothing to do with Vicky or this unexpected situation, but rather centered on a boyishly feminine form.

It was too perfectly ironic. He'd found something that gave meaning and importance to his existence, something about which he would be willing to do anything to completely win and possess. But now it was being snatched away, thrust out of reach by incidents that had their start long ago. And climaxed here.

He didn't really care about Vicky López, or about García Flynn and some "sucker" being blackmailed. Yet here he was, deeply involved, and what they decided to do to him would be carried out mercilessly, whether he cared about Vicky or not.

It was Bobbie Lee who mattered, and for this woman he would risk everything. If she hadn't left by now, if they discovered her in the bedroom, she would also be involved, and her only crime would have been her desire to be with him. It was Bobbie Lee's reaction to what was going on in this room that could doom or save him. If she reacted with violent jealousy, unreasoning emotions, then he wouldn't have a chance, and he couldn't really blame her. On the other hand, if she went for the police, they could be free of this threat in a matter of moments.

Hank was afraid to hope. He eyed the ugly hole of the .38, thinking about the death, which that black circle promised. Just the flick of a finger could project that death into his body, and everything would be finished—over.

"I see you survived our last meeting!" the gunman sneered. "It'll be different...this time around. I promise you." The man laughed, nastily. "The boss was quite unhappy with you. He's killed men for far less."

Hate burst in Hank. For a moment he wanted to leap at the man.

There was silence, then, until finally the cabin door flung open and García Flynn strutted in boldly, taking command.

García turned toward Hank and then nodded to the two men. "Take care of him—but very slow! Break him up good! I'll handle our little tramp." Then as an afterthought the man grinned, "Do him good and maybe you can have a taste of this...tramp!" The man's eyes glistened as they glanced back at Vicky. "I think you'd enjoy the twins here! What do ya think, baby?"

The woman simply glared back, saying nothing.

"Fix him good, boys and I'll promise she'll be very good to you!"

"You can't get away with this!" Hank blurted out, but he was fully aware that they could do exactly that, if he didn't think of some way of turning things to his advantage. It seemed hopeless. "What kind of man are you, anyway?"

García only grinned at Hank. Then, as his two men stepped forward, he said: "A simple business man—that's all. A man who doesn't take crap from a bum."

The man holding the gun put it in his pocket so that his fist could be free. Hank saw this movement, and had a glimmer of hope.

148

He turned to García, pleading. "Come on…for God's sake, give me a break!" he choked out in a frightened voice. Even more than just one! That's a promise!"

Hank stepped back, cringing, putting his arms out in front of him in a display of overwhelming fear. "Please, don't. I'll do anything. Anything you want. Just ask me. But please don't do this! I don't want to be hurt again. Please!"

Hank's legs began to tremble and his lips quivered, but only from his need to put on a convincing show of utter terror, an image of a desperate coward pleading for his life.

García laughed in delight. "Is this the stud that turned your hot? What a disappointing lump of crud!"

Vicky looked startled, almost disgusted at his display of naked fear. Her eyes simply said, *Be a man!*

"Bash him hard!" García ordered the men. "I want him crippled, so he'll remember me!" He pushed Vicky toward the cabin door, calling back to Hank: "And don't think it'll do you any good to go to the police. You try that and I'll see you dead. Really dead—slow and careful like. One bone at a time. Dead. Maybe the next time you'll keep it zipped."

García slammed the door, leaving him with the two hoods.

Hank kept his eyes on the men, who were now only feet away. Suddenly, without warning, he dropped to his knees, bringing his arms up before him, hands locked together as if in pleading. "Please. For God's sake have some mercy! I have money! I'll give it to you!"

"Oh, you'll need it to pay the hospital bills!" The sadistic grins on their faces revealed how they were enjoying themselves.

Hank tensed, readied every muscle as he moaned for mercy and waited for the right moment.

"He's gonna be some fun. Big man with the ladies!"

"Did Vicky ring your balls?"

"Bet she did."

"Was she worth it, lover man? Guess we'll find out soon enough!"

"That's right, García promised her as breakfast snack, after we're finished here."

They both laughed at that, grimly staring at the almost prostrate man before them. The first man was stepping forward, his large fist ready for the first blow.

That's when Hank leaped to his feet.

The next few seconds were jarred with chopping actions, as Hank slashed out his arms, hands clasped tightly together into a brutal ball. He smashed up into the groin of the first man. Then, before the other could recover from surprise, he jerked to the right, smashing his hands across the man's face.

Just as he was about to swing another blow, Hank felt his body knocked to one side. The impact of a foot snapped his head back.

Hank turned and swung at the second shadowy form, which now lunged at him. He felt a jarring pain snap his head to one side, and then another hammer into his gut. Swinging blindly, he was rewarded by the feel of a body crumbling under his fist. Again he slashed out, hammering at the face and neck until the man slumped to the floor.

Just then a pair of hands whirled Hank around, and a fist swung at his head. Automatically, without thought, Hank ducked, and at the same time grabbed hold of the arm. He twisted it, then jerked.

The man flew through the air, howling out his surprise and pain. Hank rushed after him, grabbed hold of the ugly head, and smashed it against the floor. They rolled as the man jerked around. Hank felt a knee in his groin; pain shot through his body. Somehow he managed to keep rolling over until he was once more on top of his opponent. In a red haze of pain and rage, Hank held the man's head between his clenched hands, smashing it against the floor again and again. When the other man went limp, Hank released his hold.

Agony erupted through him and he was suddenly sick, vomit flooding up his throat and past his convulsing lips. For a long time he lay there, groaning and dazed.

Finally, when the nausea had washed out of his body, he managed to stand. After a few seconds of weaving on his feet, he found himself forcing control over his body and staggering for the bedroom where he had left Bobbie Lee. He opened the door. She was gone.

150

Staggering into the bathroom, he looked at himself in the mirror. He couldn't help exposing a crooked smile. His face looked as though it had been put through a meat grinder. They'd done a pretty good job, regardless of the fact that he had come out on top.

The grin was still crookedly set on his face when a sudden dizziness whirled around him; his muscles seemed to give out, unable to support his weight. The lights dimmed and then abruptly pin-pointed into nothingness.

It seemed only a moment, but it could have been an hour, before Hank returned from the semi-unconscious stage and became aware of his surroundings once more. His first thought was of Vicky López.

Strength seeped into him and he forced his muscles to tighten and finally bring him to his feet.

He stood there groggily for a moment. Then, forcing the numbness to clear, he started toward the living room.

He had to find Vicky. There was no telling what García might do to her. Even though this wasn't his battle, he at least owed her that much for having tried to warn him.

Chapter Eight

The first place Hank thought to look was in the rooms, which Vicky must have been sharing with García. It was the only logical place the man might take her.

In the lobby he asked the desk clerk if he had seen García Flynn. The man stated that he'd gone to his rooms. Hank learned the room number, then rushed upstairs to the second floor of the lodge. Hurrying down the hall, he spotted room 2-E. He tried the doorknob. It was locked.

Sweat broke from the pores of his tense body. Then he knocked Waited

"Who is it?" García's voice inquired.

Hank knocked again, waited, and was rewarded this time by the sound of feet approaching the door. The door opened. Before García could do anything to stop him, Hank pushed in and swung a horrible blow at the man's face.

García staggered backwards, blank shock in his eyes.

Hank searched the room, then froze at the sight of Vicky López.

Vicky's lips were cut and bleeding. Her eyes were swollen, already darkening from the abuse which the man's fist had supplied. The top of her blouse had been ripped aside; the sight of her body and what the man had done to it made Hank sick with rage.

It was this shocked pause which served to give García the advantage of a few split seconds. By the time Hank had recovered and returned his attention to the man, García was leveling a small automatic at the pit of Hank's stomach.

"Don't do it!" García warned as Hank started to step forward. "I don't know how you got here or what you did to my men, but it'll be the last thing you do."

153

Hank forced a grim smile onto his face.

"What can you do with that?" he demanded, moving slowly forward. "One shot would bring too much attention. And I take it you don't want attention. So why don't you put that toy down, before you hurt somebody?"

Hank rushed the man before he could respond to the attack, smashing the side of his hand, judo style, into the side of García's neck. His other hand reached for the gun.

The gangster's strength was surprising—he did no more than groan under the attack. They struggled, violently straining for control of the weapon. García tried to point it at Hank's stomach as Hank attempted to wrench it from the other's hand.

Then suddenly he felt a knee slammed up into his groin and he slumped to the floor, doubled in agony.

García laughed.

Finally Hank regained control of himself and looked up. His voice was tight as he asked, "Now what?"

García stared at him, an expression of puzzlement settling over his fat features. "You have presented a problem. I don't know quite what to do with you. We might just wait until my men return. That would make things easier. You're becoming a real pest, and the only way to deal with a pest is to squash it. I don't like violence like that—it can get messy. But you see how things are." García Flynn shrugged his shoulders.

Hank considered rushing the man again, but realized what little chance he had of succeeding.

He looked over at Vicky and felt the sickness again. It was incredible that anyone could do a thing like that. The man must be insane. Such cruelty was beyond Hank's ability to understand. Relief washed over him that Bobbie Lee hadn't been discovered. The thought that it could have been Bobbie lying beaten like that brought on such a feeling of anguish that Hank felt the room going momentarily dark. Every muscle and nerve ached from his effort to gain control.

Finally he managed to stand, then staggered over to Vicky. One look at close range was all he needed to know she'd been seriously hurt by the man's wild beating.

"She needs a doctor," Hank gasped, turning toward García.

"That's more than you'll need in a little while."

Hank thought hard for several moments. How did García Flynn plan to get away with killing him? Yet he knew the man was capable of doing just that.

"Do you think it's worth it?" Hank finally countered.

"That has nothing to do with it. I don't need to be charged with assault and battery. What you've learned about me—from this little slut—has put us in a very awkward position. If I let you go, I don't know what you might do, who you might talk to. I'm not interested in unnecessary attention from the police. The deal I planned was for a big haul against a real class-F sucker. The man took a liking to Vicky. Well, that's out. For a little while, at least, until she gets better."

Hank looked down at her, realizing it would be a while before she got any better.

"The least you could do is untie her."

"Help yourself."

Hank worked with the belts, which García Flynn had lashed around Vicky's legs and wrists. Then, after some effort, he managed to revive her. When she finally recognized her surroundings, hate and pain worked through the muscles of her face as she turned and glared at García.

She didn't say anything for a long while. When she did, her words came out with terrible effort and strain. *"Someday...somebody will...kill you!"*

Her voice was terribly weak, and those lovely eyes fluttered, closed. A slow, shallow sigh sounded from her lungs.

The hate and complete defeat in her voice caused García to drain white. His lips compressed; with a horrible groan he leaped toward Vicky. He was already swinging the gun at her face.

Hank saw what was coming. Everything in him went blank, then turned to fiery rage.

He leaped for García, swinging. The two of them grappled like wild beasts. This time all of Hank's strength went into attacking the man's right arm. He wrapped both hands around García's wrist and twisted.

There was the sound of an explosion, then a terrible moan of agony. Hank twisted harder and García screamed, falling back as the gun clattered to the floor.

Hank turned, smashing a fist into the man's face and knocking him several feet backwards. Then he snatched up the automatic. As he did so his eyes swept toward Vicky, then hesitated. She seemed too quiet!

It didn't matter that he actually didn't love Vicky. The vital fact was that she had been a living breathing human, a passionate female who had crossed his path in life and become a part of his experience. She had offered him friendship, and tried to warn him about the danger of García's two muscle men.

She was dead. And the man responsible for her death was still alive in this room.

Hank's control snapped.

Hank's eyes narrowed and flicked toward García, who was slowly standing. He must have been groggy, for he started forward, unaware that Hank was armed. He leaped toward Hank, his arms reaching out.

Hank hesitated. And in that one instant García was upon him, beefy fists smashing into his face.

Hank staggered back under the blows, stunned, dazed. For some reason he couldn't defend himself. The gun was clutched in his hand and he couldn't pull the trigger. There was something within him that hadn't turned completely animal, which prevented him from defending himself and kept him from committing the one act, which might ruin his life 'forever'.

He had the vague intention of subduing García and then calling the police. Nothing more. Just awareness that he had to put an end to what was happening and get the authorities.

He aimed the gun, intent on killing the other man. His fingers tightened on the weapon. The man flung his arms in desperation, hitting the gun aside just as it fired.

Shocked by the sound of the gun going off caused him to freeze. The other man leaped at him and they rolled on the floor. For a moment he felt uncertain, confused. Then his arm swung, hand holding the gun connected with the other's face, slashing it aside, nose splattered red.

Hank swung again. This time the blow was carefully aimed at García's skull, smashing downward with all the strength in his arm.

There was a crunching sound, then García slumped to the floor with a gurgle and was silent.

For a long time Hank stood there dazed, unable to move, unable to understand. It seemed to him that the terrible dream had come to an end, the nightmare had finished its agony. But reality was still there, and didn't disappear.

Hank was still standing when the police burst into the room.

Epilogue

Hank Turner's mind turned away from those past few days and concentrated on his present situation. It still seemed like a nightmare, impossible to understand. Seemingly harmless events had gathered into an avalanche of horror. Mistakes. So many that he couldn't count them. If only he hadn't picked up Vicky López that night while he was drunk. If that hadn't happened he would have slowly developed his relations with Bobbie Lee, without the confusion Vicky had brought.

Even then, if he had only taken García's little pushing job and forgotten about it, things might have been different. Instead he had gone off in a temper and whacked the man around. And if only he had run away after discovering that Bobbie Lee was gone. But he hadn't considered what might happen when he went after García. Vicky's death was probably partly his own fault, too.

During the questioning Hank had learned that someone had called the police. The woman had refused to give her name, but told them to go to Hank's cabin at *Bennings Lodge*. They had gone there, found the two men and put them under temporary arrest. The sound of the shot from García's gun had drawn their attention to the Lodge. When the police arrived they'd found Hank with a gun in his hand, standing over García.

Within a couple of hours the facts appeared simple enough. There was evidence that Hank had been playing around with Vicky—witnesses had given them that information. They had reconstructed a pretty good case against him. Jealousy of García, and revenge on Vicky.

Hank's only defense had been the truth, but it wasn't

convincing. The one witness who could help was a woman who had good reason not to back up his story.

Footsteps sounded outside the room. Hank jerked his eyes in that direction.

Maybe they had found Bobbie Lee! He'd given them a good description, and the police had promised to investigate. That had been his only possible hope.

The door opened and a police officer stepped in.

"You can go now," he said. "We've found the witness you told us about; from what she's said, it's enough to back your story. But don't run off—we'll need you for the inquest."

Hank let out a deep, tired sigh, then slowly stood.

"Where is she?" he asked.

"Who?"

"Bobbie. Miss Lee."

"I don't know. Maybe in her room."

Hank rushed out of the room and down the hall, then finally down the steps to the ground floor. He had to find Bobbie, tell her how he felt. How he wanted to be with her, to know her better, and possibly, if that was the way it worked out, to marry her. He had to find out if he had a chance. In reliving the past days, he had realized how much Bobbie Lee really meant to him.

Hank ran to Bobbie's cabin, knocked at the door, waited. His heart pounded as blood raced through his body. His nerves were fired with a wildness that he'd never felt before. There wasn't any doubt about his feeling for Bobbie.

There was no answer to his knock.

Weakness flooded over him. She *had* to be there!

He pounded on the door. "Bobbie! Bobbie!"

No answer.

Turning, Hank rushed back to the lodge, into the lobby and up to the desk, where Bertha was busily looking through some papers.

"Have you seen Bobbie Lee?" he panted.

Bertha looked up at him, then shrugged her shoulders. "No. She checked out a little while ago."

"Do you know her home address? Where she lives?"

Bertha shook her head. "No."

160

"Didn't she give one when she signed in?"

Bertha smiled briefly, then shook her head again. "Just New York."

Defeated, he started for the cocktail lounge. He didn't want to drink, he didn't want to return to that hell he'd just found an escape from. But the escape was gone. His Bobbie Lee was lost.

The hell was back, and there wasn't anything left but to embrace it.

As he stepped into the lounge, it took several moments for his eyes to adjust to the dim lighting. When they did he spotted a slender boyish-looking form sitting at the bar. For a second he wasn't sure, then he couldn't believe what he was seeing.

Bobbie Lee! Just as he had seen her on that first day!

Hank rushed up to the barstool and ordered a martini. Then he turned, "accidentally" touching Bobbie with his arm.

"I'm sorry, I didn't mean to—"

He broke off. Looking into her face, into her eyes, seeing the loveliness of her, he knew beyond a doubt that there would never be another woman like her in his life, and that he could never settle for anything less.

Bobbie hesitated, then said: "I guess you didn't mean to."

"I'm afraid I did," he grinned.

She was silent for a moment. Then: "I hoped you'd find me."

"Thank God!" Hank told her. "Now what?"

Neither spoke until the martini came and Hank had sipped from it. "Why did you stay after the police brought you back?"

Bobbie turned surprised eyes in his direction. "I came back myself. I changed my mind. At first I was, mad, hurt. But I got to thinking. If a woman wants a man, she should work for him. Fight for him."

Hank was stunned to silence.

They stared into each other's eyes, then Bobbie started talking. "The moment I heard what was really going to happen, I quickly dressed, slipped out the back window, and went to call the police. I prayed to God they'd be in time. Then I left. I wanted to put as much distance between us as possible. Then I got to thinking. Well, here I am."

Hank thought for a moment, then realized exactly what he was going to do.

"Bobbie," he said, taking hold of her hand. "Come to Hollywood with me. I have connections. And if you can write at all, there's no reason we couldn't go into the picture business together."

"What are you asking?"

"What do you think?" he countered.

"I don't really know. I like it in black and white."

"I guess I'm asking you to come and be with me!" Hank took her hands in his and squeezed them gently. "This isn't the right place to be asking you something like...this."

"I don't want that kind of life, Hank," Bobbie said seriously. "I want something less temporary."

Hank laughed. Even as words formed, he was surprised at himself. He had never thought it possible to be so sure, so fast. "I'm making an offer of marriage, Bobbie. If you'll take it."

"I don't know. This is all very fast. Can I trust you?"

"Take a chance," he suggested, "life is too short to toss it all away for fear of making a mistake."

"I wonder. Are you a mistake?" She frowned, prettily.

"I don't think so. Nor are you!" he announced quite confidently. "I'll give it my all!"

"Promise?"

"Without question."

"I suppose we could...try it out for, well, size, at least once more." She glanced downwards, almost wickedly. "I think it'll fit just right! But I do want to make very certain about it!"

He had to laugh at that. "Nobody fit better than you."

"Is that love?" she wondered.

"It's a beginning!" Then without hesitation he added: "And I'm desperately in love with you, Bobbie Lee. And that's the all mighty truth!"

She looked long and hard in to his eyes, then stood,

smiling, and leaned closer to whisper in his ear. "You know, I think we were interrupted some hours ago. Let's go back to your cabin. I don't have one, you know." She smiled up at him. "Why wait for a Hollywood ending to start our lives together?"

They walked from the lounge into the chilly air. Icy wind bit their cheeks.

"Looks like snowy weather," Hank observed as they walked toward his cabin hand in hand.

"Maybe. Wouldn't it be wonderful if it would snow us in for the duration?"

They stepped into the cabin and closed the door behind them. It didn't open until the next morning, when the world was covered with a blanket of whiteness, which had fallen from the heavens during the night as an offering for the two lovers.

ABOUT THE AUTHOR

Charles Nuetzel was born in San Francisco in 1934, and writes:

"As long as I can remember I wanted to be a writer. It was a dream I never thought would materialize. But with the help of Forrest J Ackerman, who became my agent, I managed to finally make it into print.

"I was lucky enough not only in selling my work to publishers but also ending up packaging books for some of them, and finally becoming a 'publisher' much like those who had bought my first novels. From there it as a simple leap to editing not only a sci-fi anthology, but a line of sci-fi books for Powell Sci-Fi back in the 1960s. Throughout these active professional years I had the chance to design some covers and do graphic cover layouts for pocket books & magazines."

Much of his work in covers and graphics are a result of having had a father who was a professional commercial artist, and who did a number of covers for sci-fi magazines in the 1950s and later for pocket books—even for some of Mr. Nuetzel's books.

In retirement he has become involved in swing dancing, a long time lover of Big Band jazz. But more interestingly world travels have taken him (and his wife Brigitte) across the world, to Hawaii, Caribbean, Mexico, Kenya, Egypt, Peru, having a lifelong interest in ancient civilizations. His website is full of thousands of pictures taken during these trips.